I0571789

Sex Piston

Jamie Begley

Sex Piston

Copyright © 2013 by Jamie Begley
Published by Young Ink Press, LLC
Cover art by Young Ink Press, LLC

All rights reserved.

No part of this book may be reproduced in any form or by any
electronic or mechanical means including information storage
and retrieval systems, without permission in writing from the
author. The only exception is by a reviewer, who may quote
short excerpts in a review.

This book is a work of fiction. Names, characters, places, and
incidents either are products of the author's imagination or are
used fictitiously. Any resemblance to actual persons, living or
dead, events, or locales is entirely coincidental.

ISBN-13: 978-0615953144
ISBN-10: 061595314X

Prologue

Stud brought his fist up, smashing Dozer in the ribs. The beefed up brother only grunted, returning the strike with a punch to Stud's gut that had him taking a step backwards. Regaining his breath, he swung his fist, striking Dozer just under his jaw and knocking him backward before he could regain his balance. Stud then hit him on the side of his nose, sending blood flying as Dozer fell to his knees.

"That motherfucker can fight," Killyama said, admiring the two men fighting in the middle of the circle of members.

"He does all right." Sex Piston hid her appreciation at the skill that Stud used to bring down the enforcer of the Destructors down.

"Dozer should have known better than to challenge Stud. He's overworked those muscles of his to the point he's slow as shit. I could take the shithead down," Crazy Bitch said, unimpressed.

The crowd around them cheered when Stud finished off Dozer with a nasty kick to the face and then he lost consciousness. The Destructors and The Blue Horsemen converged on Stud, slapping him on his back and laughing at how easily he had taken Dozer out.

"Fuck," Sex Piston said, disappointed at the outcome of the brief fight.

"What?" Killyama said. "Don't tell me you actually thought Dozer stood a chance?"

"I was hoping. I hate it that not one of our men can beat them." Sex Piston was aggravated that the Destructors had lost every fight against The Blue Horsemen.

"I stand a better chance of beating them than any of our shitheads."

Sex Piston agreed with Crazy Bitch.

"I don't know why you don't like them. They are a hell of a lot better looking than our men. There's one or two of them I wouldn't mind doing." T.A. smiled at Bear who was standing at the edge of the crowd.

Sex Piston narrowed her eyes on her friend until she lost her smile. "You can't fuck any of them. If one of us caves, then they'll be expecting to get it off us all, and I'm not about to do any of them."

"Me either," Killyama said.

Crazy Bitch, Fat Louise and T.A. looked unhappy at Sex Piston's decision.

"Just because you're pissed off at Ace, don't mean we can't get a little something," T.A argued.

"I don't think anything of Bear's would be small, Stud's either," Fat Louise stared at Stud.

"Let's get a beer." Sex Piston turned away, walking through the crowd that had come outside to watch the fight when Dozer had challenged Stud. She actually felt kind of bad for the big man. He had been taking it pretty well that the Destructor's had been turned into a chapter of The Blue Horsemen, but then his bitch had been flirting with Stud half the night and he hadn't been able to take it anymore. His jealousy had forced him to challenge Stud to regain her attention.

She blatantly ignored Stud and his men, going back inside to find a table. Crazy Bitch grabbed them all a beer as Fat Louise kept bugging them to take her to the new restaurant that had opened in town.

"I don't want to go to Popeye's," Killyama said.

"Why not?" Fat Louise argued.

"Because if you like it, that's all we're going to be eating for the next year. I'm just going to nip it in the bud. You had us eating 'Taco Hut' so much we shitted burritos," Killyama reminded her.

"I want to go..." Fat Louise's mind was always on food.

Sex Piston drowned them out, drinking her beer as her eyes surveyed the clubhouse, seeing that Stud and his men were now at the bar. Bear's woman was in his grill so tight a fucking crowbar couldn't pry her off. Stud was ignoring the woman whose hands were all over him, but Sex Piston had no doubt that he would end up in one of the back rooms with her before the night was over.

So far, he hadn't fucked any of the Destructors' bitches, keeping his cock at home with The Blue Horsemans' women that came riding in with them on the back of their bikes. The skank with the long blond hair and tight ass was his current fuck buddy, throwing angry looks from the stool next to Stud's as the other woman made a play for him. Stud must be moving on, to ignore his bitch while playing with another one in front of her.

Sex Piston knew how that shit burned; her own man had managed to get one of the other women in the club knocked up while they were on one of their breaks, making her look like a fucking idiot. The saddest part was she hadn't cared. She was actually glad knowing that now she wouldn't go back to him even if he begged her, and he had been begging, but she had her standards. She wasn't about to come between a man and his baby's mama.

"We need to talk," Ace said, coming up to her table.

"No, we don't," Sex Piston said, finishing her beer.

"Summer doesn't mean a damn thing to me. Her

having my kid isn't going to change how I feel about you."

"You don't give a fuck about me or your dick never would've come out of your pants. We're done. Now get the fuck away from me." She stared back at him, ice dripping from her voice.

Joker came up beside his friend. "Crazy Bitch, let's go home."

"I told you last night I was done with your ass. Your shit better be out of my house before I get home or I'll give it to Goodwill. I'm sick of supporting your lazy ass. Go find another bitch stupid enough to pay your fucking bills." Crazy Bitch glared at her ex.

"I'm looking for a job," Joker whined.

"I hear Popeye's is hiring," Crazy Bitch mocked. The women at the table burst out laughing at the men.

Joker made to grab Crazy Bitch, but Sex Piston jerked his hand away before he could touch her. "Don't fucking touch her," she snarled.

"She's my old lady; I'll touch her if I want to, you bitch from hell. Ace should have shown you who was boss years ago."

"Yeah, well, he would have to have a dick for that to happen." The women at the table couldn't help but laugh again. Ace turned bright red, grabbing Sex Piston's arm. Sex Piston grabbed her beer bottle about to brain the fucker…

"Let her go, Ace." Ace let go of Sex Piston as soon as he heard Stud's voice.

"See, what did I tell you? No dick," Sex Piston taunted.

"Shut up, Sex Piston." Stud didn't take his eyes off Joker and Ace. "You two need to leave until you cool down."

"You throwing me out of my own club?" Joker asked in astonishment.

"It's my club now, and yeah, I'm telling you to leave." Stud didn't say anything else as he waited for the two men to follow his orders or challenge him.

"Let's go, Joker. Neither one of these bitches are worth fighting over." Ace walked away, heading toward the club door. Joker hesitated; it was harder to walk away from his meal ticket, yet without Ace to back him up, his cowardice showed and he followed behind his friend.

After they left, Stud stood staring down at the table of women.

"If you're waiting for thanks, you're not going to get it. I could have handled that pussy," Sex Piston said as she glared up at her new club president.

"Watch how you talk to me, Sex Piston," Stud warned her.

Sex Piston started to snap back, but bit her tongue for once. She had promised her pops she wouldn't challenge the asshole. She managed to keep her mouth shut, turning to talk to Killyama and insulting him by ignoring his presence.

The bitches gave him gloating smiles as he returned to the bar.

"T.A., get a bottle of Tequila. Let's celebrate those two assholes being out of our life," Crazy Bitch said.

T.A. got up and went to the bar, coming back a few minutes later with a full bottle and five glasses.

Sex Piston poured herself a large glass before passing the bottle on to her friends. Taking a swallow of the burning liquor, she wondered how long she was going to be able to keep her promise to her pops. That asshole deserved to be put in his place and she was just the bitch to do it.

* * *

"I'm going to do it," Bear said, setting his beer down on the counter.

"Do what?" Stud asked, turning to his vice-president. His eyes went in the direction that Bear was obviously watching.

The five women must have gone onto the dance floor after finishing the empty tequila bottle still sitting at their table. He hadn't noticed with his attention on the blond that had been attached to his hip for the last hour. She had been trying to lure him into one of the back rooms for a blowjob for the last hour; however his dick had shown no interest.

The best part about being the president of the Blue Horsemen was the pussy. Contrarily, the worst part of the job was the pussy. Women were constantly trying to get his attention, wanting to become his old lady or just be able to brag about having fucked him. He had learned early just how manipulative the bitches in the club could be. All except for one, Sex Piston. She didn't bother trying to manipulate anyone, she merely steamrolled over them.

He had seen her on and off for the last several years when the Destructors and the Blue Horsemen partied together.

Sex Piston's father, Skulls, and he had met seven years ago during a run in with another club. They had sided together to get rid of the encroaching biker club that was stealing and doing drug runs, blaming it on their clubs. When they had banded together, the rival biker club had left town with fewer members than when they had arrived.

Sex Piston had been nineteen and feisty as hell. Now, at twenty-six, she more than deserved her name. Her five-foot-six, curvy body was encased in tight, black leather pants with a leather vest that was laced up the front with her breasts threatening to overflow the corseted top. All the brothers were constantly staring, trying to see the pink of her nipples, yet they only managed to get threats for those high-heeled, biker boots to be shoved up their asses.

"I'm going to have that bitch in my bed tonight," Bear bragged.

"Which one?" Stud asked, picking up his beer, deliberately keeping his body loose.

Bear looked at him as if he was insane. "T.A. I'm man enough to admit I couldn't handle the other four."

"Not even Fat Louise?" Stud smiled at Bear's horror-stricken expression.

"Nope, she's more interested in food than dick," Bear said, hiking his jeans up before moving toward the dance floor.

Stud laughed. "I've got to watch this."

Bear threw him a confident look before walking over to the dance floor. He tried to sidle up next to T.A., but a remark from Crazy Bitch had him turning on the heel of his boot, returning to his side.

"Fucking bitch. You have to get them under control, Stud. They're making fools out of us." Bear angrily picked up his beer.

"It's only been a couple of weeks. They'll adjust," Stud said.

"Those bitches aren't planning on adjusting, they're planning on neutering us and doing a good job of it," Bear snapped back, his face red.

"Give it time." Stud ignored Bear's angry remarks, knowing his anger, and those of his brothers, came from being unable to get in the women's pants. Most of his men had already had their eyes on their particular favorites, but not a one of them stood a chance in hell.

"What's that asshole doing?" Bear said as Pike took his chance with the women. His seductive expression turned angry when Killyama danced close, using her body to bump him away from Fat Louise. Aggravated when he almost tripped over another brother and his old lady, he retreated to his own table who all jeered at him as he returned unsuccessfully.

"The only way those bitches are going to take any of us on is if Sex Piston lets them. One of us would have to take that werebitch on, and I don't know a man here who's going to let that bitch put a hand on his balls," Bear said glumly as he took a swig of his beer.

Stud listened to his vice president as he watched the bitches leave the dance floor as T.A. went to the bar for another bottle of Tequila.

A smile came to his lips as a thought occurred to him; a way he could take care of one of the club's biggest problems in one night. Bear was wrong; there was one man in the club more than willing to let Sex Piston near his balls.

* * *

Sex Piston rolled over. Her freaking head was ready to explode. Carefully rising up on her elbow, she put her hand to her head, pushing back the tangled mess so that she could see in the dim room. She groaned, recognizing one of the bedrooms in the clubhouse. The cool air hitting her naked breasts had her looking down at her bareness at the same time she realized that she was just as naked under the sheet around her lower body.

A movement at her side had her head turning, staring down at the man lying beside her naked. His sleeping face was easily recognizable as Sex Piston gasped in shock, pulling the sheet up to cover herself. Carefully, she slid to the edge of the bed before getting to her feet as silently as possible. She wrapped the sheet around her, looking quickly for her clothes. She took a cautious step forward, trying to find…

"Going somewhere? I thought you wanted another round before you left." Stud's amused voice came from the rumpled bed.

Sex Piston tensed, humiliated at what she had allowed to happen. Gathering her shattered dignity, she turned back to face him.

"Asshole, where are my clothes?"

Chapter One

Stud paused for a second, his eyes on Sex Piston's curves, which were clearly outlined under the white sheet, before reaching down beside the bed and tossing Sex Piston her clothes. They landed on the bed beside him.

She tossed him an aggravated look before reaching out to grab them. Like a striking snake, Stud grabbed her arm, jerked her down onto the bed and then rolled over her, trapping her struggling body underneath his.

"Let me go," Sex Piston demanded.

"What's the hurry?" Stud asked, nuzzling her neck.

She tried to put her knee in his balls, but he insinuated himself between her thighs, notching his cock against her pussy with just the thin sheet separating them.

"Get off me." She then went at him with her nails.

Stud laughed, catching her hands and raising them over her head. "Now, is this any way to repay me for those orgasms I gave you last night?" His taunts fueled her anger.

Her green eyes spit their fury at him. "It isn't going to happen, Stud. The tequila has worn off. I should have known Blue Horsemen were the type to take advantage of a drunken woman."

"Sex Piston, I didn't pour that tequila down your throat, you did that all by yourself. I'm not ashamed to admit when you were rubbing your ass all over my dick that I wasn't strong enough to say no. Now that I think about it, you took advantage of me." She wanted to strangle him with that self-righteous bullshit spewing from his mouth.

Her blazing green eyes looked up into his caramel colored ones, searching for the truth. She was woman enough to admit she knew she was drinking too much, but Fat Louise was supposed to stay sober to make sure shit like this didn't happen. She had obviously failed. Sex Piston was going to kick her ass as soon as she took care of Stud.

Turning her head toward his shoulder, she sank her teeth deep into his muscled flesh, biting hard.

"Bitch." Stud rolled away, his hand going to the painful mark left by her bite.

"When I say move, fucking move." Sex Piston used the opportunity to grab her clothes and rise to her feet while throwing him a triumphant look.

Ignoring his presence, she threw down the sheet and got dressed, uncaring of her nakedness. Planting her ass on the side of the bed, she put on her boots, aware that he was watching every move she made.

"Your tits are the best I've ever seen, and your ass is even better. Ace is a stupid bastard to mess around on you." Sex Piston paused putting on her boots. His compliments soothed a hurt she had denied to everyone, including herself.

Stud got out of the bed naked and walked around the bed to face her. Sex Piston was unable to prevent herself from salivating at his muscular body. Ace had let his go with one too many beers; he had a paunch to prove it and flabby arms where there should have been muscles. Stud's dick also put Ace's to shame. She shook her head, coming to the conclusion that Stud had earned his name for more than one reason.

"Come a step closer to me and those three kids of yours will be the last kids you'll be able to have." Stud ignored her threat, moved closer to her and then reached down to pick up his t-shirt lying on the floor beside her foot.

"Sex Piston, that mouth of yours might put the fear of God into everyone else, but to me, it just reminds me it was on my dick last night." Stud went to the foot of the bed and picked up his jeans, his firm ass flexing as he put them on. Giving her a mocking look, he shoved his dick into the pants before zipping them up. He put on his t-shirt next before sitting on the bed to put on his boots, not bothering to look for his socks. He grabbed his jacket and went to the bedroom door, waiting for her to brush her fingers through her thick hair.

"What are you doing?" Sex Piston paused when she noticed he was watching.

"Waiting to give you a ride home," he explained with a smirk.

"No you're not. Go on out and leave. I don't need a ride home." She wasn't about to leave the room at the same time as him. If she was lucky, no one had seen them enter the room together. She was already furious at herself for not remembering the night before, but she damn sure wasn't about to compound the mistake of walking out of the room with him.

"How are you going to get home?" Stud questioned.

"I'll call Killyama," Sex Piston answered as she searched through her clothes for her cell phone.

"Good luck with that; Bear was supposed to give them all rides home last night. They weren't in any better shape than you were."

Finding her phone in her pants pocket, she called her crew one at a time, receiving no answers. Becoming more aggravated with each call, Stud merely leaned against the bedroom wall, waiting for her to come to the same conclusion as him. That she would have to accept his offer of a ride.

Using her internet, she looked up the number for a cab and pushed the number in. When the dispatcher answered, she gave the address. Stud strode forward and took the phone away, cancelling the cab.

"Fucker, give me back my phone."

Stud put the phone in his back pocket. Then, taking her arm, he propelled her through the doorway, ignoring her demand to leave her alone. "Let's go, Sex Piston. I'm giving you a ride."

She tried to jerk away, but it was useless as she found herself being led down the hallway into the main room of the club. She quit struggling when she saw several members still sitting around the bar, having done an all-nighter.

Bear, Stud's vice president, was one of the men. His snicker had Sex Piston wishing she had Crazy Bitch's bat.

"I'll be back in a few minutes, Bear. I'm going to give Sex Piston a ride home," Stud informed his brother, still ushering Sex Piston through the club.

Sex Piston kept her mouth closed, continuing on outside with him since the rat bastard gave her no choice. Jerking her arm free once they were outside, she gave in and stood next to the back of his bike.

"What's the hurry?" he mocked her with a knowing look in his eyes.

"Just take me home," Sex Piston snapped.

Stud got on his bike, and Sex Piston paused. She had never ridden behind anyone other than her pops and Ace. So, wanting to get home before anyone else saw her, she let only her fingertips grasp his waist.

"Grab on, Sex Piston," Stud said as he pulled out onto the road. Sex Piston ignored him, causing Stud to pull over onto the shoulder of the road. "Either hold onto me right or we'll sit here until you do."

Sex Piston's hands took a firmer grip on his waist. As soon as she did, Stud pulled back onto the road.

"Good girl," he praised, not taking his eyes off the road.

She bit back her smartass comment, not wanting to prolong the torture of being in his irritating company.

Sex Piston was thankful that there wasn't much traffic out so early in the morning and no one she knew saw her on the back of Stud's bike. It didn't matter anyway; she was sure Bear's big mouth would spread the word about her spending the night with Stud.

As soon as Stud pulled into her driveway and came to a stop, Sex Piston jumped off the bike turning to go inside her house, but Stud's hand snagged her wrist, preventing her.

"No kiss goodbye?"

"Yeah, you can kiss my ass goodbye," Sex Piston said, struggling against his hold.

"Now, for some reason I'm thinking you didn't appreciate my efforts last night. Let me just remind you."

Stud pulled her closer to him, plastering her against his chest. His hand buried in her hair and he used it to bring her face down to his level. His mouth fastened onto hers and then his tongue delved into her mouth despite her determination to keep him out.

Sex Piston froze at his expertise. Her body tightened in pleasure as he explored her mouth, stroking her tongue before pulling back with a final stroke on her bottom lip. The son of a bitch who had always stared at everyone with eyes that said he had done it all... well, he had done it all, and it showed in his kiss. Stud had shown her a brief glimpse of what he had to offer and, holy hell, she was tempted.

Sex Piston straightened when it was obvious he was done.

"Later." His nonchalant goodbye helped her regain her senses.

She turned on her heel, leaving him without saying anything. Her front door was unlocked, so she unceremoniously went inside her parents' house, quickly closing the door and leaning back against it.

"Damn."

Chapter Two

Sex Piston was cooking dinner when her crew showed up later that day. Crazy Bitch and Killyama were the first to saunter into the kitchen, both looking hung over from the night before.

Sex Piston put her ham in the oven before turning to them.

"Don't give me that look," Killyama said. "Fat Louise let us all down. We woke up on the pool table with those assholes staring at us. I tried to call her, but she's not answering. When I see her, I am going to kick her ass."

"When I get done with her, she's not going to be able to eat at Popeye's because her jaw is going to be wired shut," Sex Piston said, putting some vegetables together for a quick side dish. She loved to cook, but when she was upset, she cooked enough to feed an army, which good because her friends were making themselves at home.

Her ma, Sizzle, breezed into the kitchen, coming to a stop when she saw her daughter and crew in the kitchen. "Good, you already started dinner. I was going to cook, but this works out even better. I asked company over so make sure you make enough."

"We'll have enough. Who did you invite?" Sex Piston asked.

Her ma ignored her, looking in the oven at the ham cooking then raising a lid on one of the saucepans bubbling slowly on the stove. Replacing the lid gently, as if she was the one to make it, she wiped her hands on a kitchen cloth. "I'm going to go get changed."

Sex Piston raised a brow at that, Sizzle never dressed up when she invited friends over.

She stared at the amount of food on the stove then at Sex Piston's crew sitting familiarly at the table. "Where's Fat Louise?"

"That's what we would like to know," Sex Piston answered her grimly.

"Well, make sure when she gets here that she doesn't eat all the food," Sizzle said, going out the door as she gave Sex Piston a rolling of her eyes, which was her mother not so subtly warning her not to let them eat all the food either.

"Wonder who she invited?" Crazy Bitch asked.

"Don't know, don't care." Sex Piston shrugged. "I have enough to feed everyone." She had planned to use the leftovers for her pops lunch throughout the week. If there wasn't any left, then she would just come up with something else.

She made crust enough for two pies, deciding to make extra for dessert. She had learned to cook while still in grade school or they would have starved to death. Her mother was a terrible cook and Diamond had been more interested in books than helping in the kitchen. Both Diamond and their father were always content with the sandwiches her ma made when she made dinner, not Sex Piston.

"I hope whoever it is doesn't eat much, the food smells good," Killyama said.

"I'm sure you'll manage to get your fair share," Sex

Piston assured her as she spooned the chocolate filling into the pie shells before putting on the meringue.

She was taking both pies back out of the oven when her ma came back into the kitchen with an excited expression on her face. "They're here." Walking to the refrigerator, she pulled out three beers and two sodas before going back out into the other room.

"I have to see this," Crazy Bitch said, getting up from her seat at the kitchen table and walking out into the other room. When she didn't come back for several minutes, Killyama and T.A. got up from the table; their curiosity getting the better of them.

Sex Piston finished placing the food into serving dishes while waiting for her friends to come back. When they didn't, she became curious despite herself. She, too, went into the other room.

Walking through the dining room, she came to a stop in the doorway of the living room.

Her mother was sitting with a little girl on her lap. The toddler was all dressed up with frilly hair bows in her curly blond hair and wearing a bright pink dress. Two other children, who seemed about eleven-years-old, were sitting on the couch, staring daggers at her crew. The two girls were obviously twins and were not impressed with her friends' unfriendly attitudes.

Stud was standing by the window, talking to Skulls and ignoring the stare down going on behind his back.

Her mother looked up, seeing her standing by the doorway. "Is dinner ready?" Sizzle asked, unnecessarily straightening the baby's dress.

Sex Piston nodded before turning away and walking back into the kitchen. Picking up the ham, she packed it out to the dining room table as the rest of her crew began to help bring out the rest of the meal. Going back into the kitchen, she picked up the pitcher of tea before going back to the table.

The only chair left at the table was the one by Stud.

Throwing her friends a dirty look, she reluctantly sat down.

Her mother started passing the food around the table. Stud had no problem filling his plate. Her mother, Sex Piston had noticed, had pulled out hers and Diamond's old highchair and sat his daughter in it. Her ma had sat the highchair next to her and was giving the little girl small bites of food.

"This brings back memories for me, Stud. Thanks for bringing your children to dinner." Her ma was so sweet it grated on Sex Piston's nerves.

Stud gave her mother a charming smile, which Sex Piston rolled her eyes at. Her mother threw her a sharp look, which had her dropping her eyes back to her plate. Her ma might come across as sickeningly sweet to Stud, but she would rip her head off if she felt Sex Piston was being rude at her dinner table.

"Don't you have any normal food?" one twin asked rudely. She picked up the ham slice on her fork, wiggling it like a worm on a hook.

Sex Piston opened her mouth, but shut it at Stud's sharp rebuke to his daughter. "Meri, apologize now."

The girl raised rebellious eyes to Sex Piston, but followed her father's order. "Sorry." The mini witch was lying through the braces on her teeth.

Sex Piston didn't acknowledge the girl's apology. The girl needed to realize who the Queen of Bitches was. She was going to get a quick lesson if she kept it up.

"The girls would just eat nuggets and hamburgers if I let them. The woman that's been keeping them after school has been feeding them too much junk food. That's why I decided to find another sitter."

Sex Piston kept eating her food, not interested in who he hired to keep his kids.

"I'm looking forward to keeping them, Stud." Her ma spoke just as Sex Piston took a bite of ham. She started to choke, so Stud reached behind her, slapping her on the

18

back.

It took several minutes to clear her airway before she could choke out her surprised words. "Quit hitting me," Sex Piston hissed at Stud. Taking a drink of water, she was finally able to clear her throat.

"You okay?" Stud asked in amusement.

"I'm fine," she snapped at him. "Ma, you can't keep them."

Her mother's hurt face stared back at her. "I certainly can. I've been bored to death since I've retired. Having this little girl around will keep me busy. The older two are in school all day, so I'll just be picking them up from school and keeping them until Stud gets off work."

Sex Piston shook her head. Her mom was wonderful with kids, but she had a little problem when she attempted to keep them for any length of time.

"Ma." She shook her head at her mother.

"Sex Piston, your mother has decided to do this. Leave it alone," Skulls intervened, giving his wife a smile of reassurance.

She threw her father a disbelieving look.

"If it's going to cause a problem, I can find another sitter," Stud broke into the glares between father and daughter.

"It's not a problem," Sizzle hastily assured Stud.

Sex Piston closed her mouth with a snap. She looked at the little toddler sitting in the highchair. She hated to admit it because she disliked Stud, but the little girl was freaking cute. She had a head full of blond, curly hair and plump, rosy cheeks with a little bow mouth. The kid could be on Christmas cards.

The not so little girls on the other side of the table, giving her venomous looks, were cute also, but Sex Piston could tell discipline hadn't been a big factor in their lives. She personally didn't have a problem with that, but it would give her mother one of her migraines.

They needed to be around her pop for a week or two.

He hadn't hesitated to set her and her sister straight when they had gotten out of hand. Of course, she had learned to avoid punishments as she had gotten older, but she still knew enough not to act like an outright bitch until she was much older, beyond the age of his swatting hand.

Sex Piston saw Killyama chew her food as she watched the family argue before the woman swallowed and spoke up. "Didn't you lose Sex Piston when she was that kid's age?"

Sizzle looked at Killyama in reproach. "That wasn't my fault. I thought she had gone to the store with Skulls."

Killyama nodded her head. "She wandered the neighborhood for an hour before a neighbor brought her home."

"She was a rambunctious child," her mother said in her own defense.

Killyama sat back in her chair. Sex Piston almost smiled at her friend as she reminded her mother just how bad she was at watching kids. "Then there was the time she had pneumonia because you forgot her in the car when it was freezing outside."

"I didn't forget her. Someone called. And it was only a couple of minutes."

Killyama shook her head. "When you kept your niece's baby, how long did that last?"

Her ma stiffened. "How was I supposed to know the kid still wore diapers? He was old enough to be potty trained."

"He was a year old," Killyama answered.

"He was big for his age," her mother snapped.

"Star isn't potty trained," Meri said, looking at her father in concern.

"Of course she's not," her mother crooned to the toddler sitting next to her. "Meri, I will take good care of your sister. You and Keri don't have to worry. I was much younger then, I'm older now."

"Thirty-two wasn't young," Crazy Bitch joined in the

conversation.

Her ma was beginning to look frustrated. "Sex Piston and her friends don't need to worry, everything will be fine," she again reassured Stud whose amusement at Sex Piston's reaction had disappeared.

"Her name is Sex Piston?" Keri asked.

"That's her nickname. She picked it up at school. It's just become a habit to use it." Her mother turned to Sex Piston. "Maybe it would be best if we just use your name when the kids are around."

Sex Piston choked on her food again. "Don't—"

"After all, Norma is a beautiful name. It was my mother's."

Even her father winced and both twins shot her glances of sympathy at the mention of her name.

"Sex Piston's nickname is fine," Stud said, trying not to smile. "I don't think it will traumatize the girls using it."

"Okay, now that's settled, let's finish eating. She made dessert."

Sex Piston went into the kitchen to get the pies, looking up when she noticed Stud had followed her into the room.

"If you say one thing, I'll kick your ass," Sex Piston threatened with the pie in her hand.

Stud put his hands up in surrender. "I just came in to offer help."

Sex Piston thrust the pies at him, which he hastily grabbed. She picked up dessert plates and forks before leaving him with no choice but to follow.

The pies were demolished instantly and then her parents and Stud drank coffee afterwards as Sex Piston and her crew cleaned the table and did the dishes. When they finished, Sex Piston went back into the living room where her parents and Stud were discussing the Destructors while his kids dozed on the couch.

"We're going to take off, Ma. Be back later," Sex Piston informed her mother as she grabbed her leather jacket from the closet.

"Where are you going?" she asked casually.

"Fat Louise isn't answering her phone; we're going to go see why." Sex Piston threw Stud a dirty look, which he returned with a face devoid of expression.

"Probably still sleeping," he said, staring back at her.

"Probably, but I need to have a talk with her." *Not to mention, kick that ass she is so proud of.*

Stud smiled. "See you later then."

Sex Piston paused on the way out of the door, restraining herself from giving him an earful because of the children present. Rudely not responding, she left with her friends, knowing that if she didn't get away from the man, she was going to smack him upside his head.

Fat Louise better have a good explanation of how Sex Piston had ended up in bed with that man. The woman was a serious fuck up, but they had counted on her to remain sober and watch their backs and she had let them all down.

Sex Piston would have rather woke up next to any club member than Stud. They had been silently challenging each other since he had taken over as President. He thought that he had won the first battle. The only battle he had won was one the fucker hadn't even known about.

Chapter Three

Sex Piston banged her fist on Fat Louise's door. It took several minutes for Fat Louise to answer the door. Her blond hair was a mess and she was still wearing the same clothes she was wearing the night before.

"What...?" she managed to get out before Sex Piston pushed her backwards into her mother's apartment.

"Bitch, I'm giving you one chance to tell me how I woke up in Stud's bed and the rest of them sleeping on the pool table."

"I don't know. T.A. told me it was her turn to not drink."

"I didn't. I told you it was my turn *to* drink. You had your mind on your stomach more than watching our backs." T.A. glared at her friend.

Tears welled into Fat Louise's eyes. "I'm sorry, I made a mistake."

Sex Piston eased off her friend as always. She had fucked up, but she was going to make it up to them.

"You're going to be at my house at eight in the morning," Sex Piston told her. "Ma is going to babysit Stud's kids for a while."

"She can't babysit," Fat Louise stated in disbelief.

"I know that. That's where you come in. Tell mom you're waiting for me to get off work."

"At eight in the morning? She's a space cadet, but she's not that stupid," Fat Louise argued.

"Then make up something else. I don't care, but I don't want Ma left alone with the kids. Got it?"

Fat Louise nodded her head. "We'll be okay then? You won't be mad anymore?" she cajoled. The woman couldn't handle the thought of anyone holding a grudge against her.

Sex Piston sighed. "We won't be mad anymore, but you should have had our backs."

Fat Louise nodded. "I'm sorry. I'll make it up to you. But I still think it was T.A.'s turn."

T.A. gave her friend a hard shove. "It was your fucking turn! How did you get home?"

"Bear drove me home last night when you guy's all got shit-faced and didn't want to leave. Did something happen?"

"Sex Piston fucked Stud," T.A. answered.

"Was he any good?" Fat Louise asked breathlessly.

"How do I know? I don't remember a damn thing," Sex Piston snapped.

"If you remember, will you let me know? I've been curious. I mean, he really seems like he would know how to fuck really good."

Sex Piston clenched her hands by her side to hold herself back from punching her friend. "You'll be the first to know if I ever remember what happened last night," Sex Piston threatened her friend.

Fat Louise finally got the message that she was stepping on fragile ground and shut-up.

"What were we doing when you left?" Killyama asked.

"Sitting at the bar, taking shots," Fat Louise answered. "I tried to get you to leave with me and Bear, but you told me no. Stud was with several brothers playing pool in the back room."

Sex Piston again tried to prod her own memory, but came up with a blank. "You guys remember anything?"

Their "no" was unanimous.

"The last thing I remember is getting that third bottle of Tequila," Killyama said thoughtfully.

"Three bottles?" Fat Louise asked, wide-eyed. "That might explain why you guys don't remember anything."

"I don't remember the third bottle," Sex Piston admitted.

"You remember more than me. I don't remember the second one," Crazy Bitch confessed.

"If someone was doing her job, it wouldn't have mattered how many bottles we had drunk," Killyama reminded them.

"I'm sorry I let you guys down. It won't happen again."

"You're right about that. The next time it's your turn, I'll drink beer." Killyama snapped.

Fat Louise's lips trembled. "I'll make it up to you; you'll see."

Sex Piston sighed. She had never been able to stay mad at Fat Louise, despite her many screw ups. "Like I said, you can repay me by helping Ma watch those kids."

"I'll be at your house bright and early, Sex Piston. I won't let you down again. How many kids does he have?"

"Three," Crazy Bitch answered.

"Are they nice?" Fat Louise asked, eager to please.

"You're going to love them," Sex Piston lied.

* * *

Stud handed his daughter over to a heavy-eyed Sizzle, who gave him a cheerful smile. Sex Piston was leaning against the doorway, drinking a cup of coffee and giving him her usual fuck-off glare, which he ignored.

Placing Star's diaper bag on the couch, he leaned over to kiss his daughter's cheek. "Later, baby girl."

Giving Sex Piston a smile, he left his daughter giggling.

Stud went back outside and climbed into his truck. Aware Sex Piston was watching from the window, he drove off without glancing in her direction. Going around the block, he took several turns around the neighborhood before parking behind a truck several doors down from Sex Piston's house.

Five minutes later, Sex Piston came out and got on her bike. He admired the way she maneuvered the bike onto the road, riding off in the opposite direction from him.

Skulls had already left for his job, and Stud knew that Sex Piston was heading to open her beauty salon. He was about to pull out and return to her mother's house and get his daughter when the roar of a car coming down the road caught his attention. A familiar green car pulled into the driveway of Sex Piston's house.

Fat Louise hurriedly got out of the car and went to the door, knocking impatiently. Sizzle answered the door with Star in her arms. Fat Louise held her arms out for his daughter and Star went immediately to her. Fat Louise stepped into the house and Sizzle closed the door behind her.

Stud sat there for an hour, making sure he was right that Fat Louise was Star's new babysitter whether Sex Piston's mom knew it or not.

He started his truck, whistling. He now had the bitches where he wanted them; it was up to Star to do the rest.

* * *

Stud sat in Rabbit's borrowed truck, across the street from the school, watching the schoolhouse. The line for pick-ups was long.

He whistled to himself as he watched Killyama pulling up to pick up his girls. The unfortunate Assistant Principal checked her list in fright as Killyama waited. Finally, she allowed Meri and Keri to get into the backseat of the car.

Stud watched as the car pulled out of the school parking lot in the direction of Sex Piston's home.

He made himself wait a couple of hours before going to pick up his girls. Sex Piston's whole crew was there, trying to manage them.

Star was crying while Crazy Bitch tried to change her diaper. Meri was playing a game on Killyma's phone while she tried to get it back, and Keri was screaming at Fat Louise for eating her snack. Sizzle sat on the couch, talking on her cell phone while the chaos surrounded her.

Stud opened his mouth to calm the situation down when Sex Piston came in the door behind him. Taking one look, she took control. Going to Star, she leaned over, expertly taping the diaper closed then lifting the tearful baby and balancing Star on her hip, swaying her into silence. Then she went to the struggling Killyama and Meri. She reached between them, snagging the phone and handing it to a furious Killyama.

"Shut up!" Silence ensued into the room at Sex Piston's yell.

"She downloaded a six dollar game onto my phone!" Killyama said, her fingers trying to clear her phone.

"Stud, give her six bucks." Sex Piston held out her hand.

Stud didn't argue as he took a ten out of his wallet and placed it in her waiting hand.

"She ate my snack," Keri accused Fat Louise.

"Go make her a new one, Fat Louise," Sex Piston told her food addict friend.

"She didn't want the darn thing until I ate it," she said, throwing Keri a reproachful look, but still went into the kitchen to make her another sandwich.

"Don't bother; I'll fix them dinner when we get them home," Stud interrupted the women.

Sex Piston's mom hung up the phone, smiling broadly at Stud. "They're precious, Stud. The day couldn't have gone better."

Sex Piston and her crew watched as Sizzle gathered the girls' things, gushing compliments the whole time. Stud packed the girls' backpacks and Star's diaper bag outside to his truck with Keri and Meri following meekly behind him. Sex

Piston's friends breathed a sigh of relief as Sex Piston put Star's jacket on the wiggling child.

She turned to pack the child outside to Stud only to find him standing behind her. Handing him his squirming daughter, she took a quick step back, but came up short when Star's hand tangled in her hair. She reached to untangle the child's fingers just as Stud did. The brush of his fingers against her sparked a jolt of sensation that she disguised by lowering her lashes and moving away.

Sex Piston went into the kitchen, not waiting for Stud to leave. She pulled together a quick dinner for her parents and her crew. The mundane task eased her tension.

She came to the conclusion she was going to have to avoid Stud. It should be easy to do; she would spend less time at the Destructors' club, and come home after he picked up his girls. She was sure she was only feeling the leftover attraction to their spending the night together. Even though she didn't remember it, obviously her body did.

She felt better once she had a plan of action. That was how she solved all her problems—determined what the problem was then developed a plan of action that took care of it.

Stud was a big problem that she had no intention of making more complicated. Her course of action would be to stay the hell away from the sexy biker, which would keep her traitorous body from reacting to his presence. The only thing to do was to make sure Stud followed her plan by staying the hell away from her.

Chapter Four

As Sex Piston watched her parents ride away on her pop's bike after their wedding ceremony, she thought about taking off like her sister had minutes before.

"Let's Par-tay," Crazy Bitch said, going back inside the Destructors' clubhouse. Killyama, T.A. and Fat Louise waited to see what Sex Piston wanted to do.

"Sounds good to me. So there is no misunderstanding this time, I'll stay dry," Sex Piston said, heading back inside, wishing she had brought a change of clothes. The yellow dress her ma had wanted her to wear for her wedding made her feel too prissy for her own taste.

Crazy Bitch had already managed to snag them one of the few tables with beers waiting for them. Sex Piston took a seat, ignoring the beer. The music was loud, playing off the noise of the big crowd, and the dance floor was already packed.

Bear asked T.A. to dance. She looked at Sex Piston for approval.

Sex Piston shrugged her shoulders, leaving it up to her. T.A. smiled at her with an I'm-gonna-be-bad smile, which Sex Piston returned with a raised brow.

Bear might think he had a sure thing, but Sex Piston knew her friend well. If he got any vajayjay off T.A., he was going to have to work for it. Everyone thought that T.A. was an easy lay, when she was the exact opposite. She would occasionally give it out, but they had to show the selective woman they were worth admitting to her bed.

Rabbit was next, claiming Fat Louise for a dance. She jumped to her feet, giving him not much of a choice since she took him by the hand and led him to the dance floor.

The three remaining women stared at each other before getting to their feet and moving to the dance floor. Sex Piston loved to dance, moving her body to the beat of the music. Killyama was the best dancer of the three, letting her guard down to flow with the music. Crazy Bitch was good, too, dancing to the music seductively, showing off her curvy body that drew more than one male's eye.

Sex Piston felt someone move up behind her, his hand sliding across the soft material of her dress as he pressed on her flat stomach until she felt a hard chest against her back. She stiffened when his hips pressed against her ass.

"Back off."

"Not a chance," Stud answered her demand.

She tried to pull away when he buried his face in her neck, but he pressed harder against her stomach, pushing her tighter against him. Sex Piston felt his hardening cock against her backside while he kept moving them to the music.

"Having trouble hearing her?" Killyama asked, taking a step forward. Pike, one of the Blue Horsemen that had come from West Virginia with Stud, stepped forward, blocking her from interfering and then moving her away with an arm around her waist.

"You having a problem with Pike? Because she's going to kick his ass," Sex Piston murmured as Stud's lips trailed to the back of her neck. She shivered at the sensations he was arousing in her.

Crazy Bitch kept dancing, waiting for Sex Piston to

make up her mind. She had confidence her friend was more than able to handle Stud.

When his fingers spread across her abdomen, his thumb brushed against her tightened nipple. She jerked herself out of his hold, moving to Crazy Bitch's side, placing her between Stud and herself.

His eyes burned into her, daring her to come back to him. "Scared, Sex Piston?" he taunted her.

Those were fighting words to her. "I'm not afraid of fucking you, Stud. Just did it once, and can't remember shit about it, so you're not worth doing again."

"I don't mind refreshing your memory," Stud offered.

"You remind me of my sister. She believes in zombies, and you actually believe I would let you touch me sober." Sex Piston started dancing again with Crazy Bitch, deliberately making her moves seductive, teasing him with what he couldn't have again.

Stud's eyes narrowed on her swaying body as Pike crashed to the floor behind Sex Piston, holding his crotch. Sex Piston didn't have to turn around to know exactly what her girl had done. Killyama returned to her side, throwing Stud a triumphant smile.

Sex Piston looked at the crowded club. Seeing Oz, she gave him a luring smile in which he immediately responded to, joining her on the dance floor. Sex Piston began dancing with him, grinding herself against his leg which had slid between hers.

Stud gave her a grim promise, "The next time I fuck you, you'll be sober and begging me."

"Go fuck those bitches that are waiting for you at the bar and leave me the hell alone." Sex Piston swayed, giving him her back.

Stud left the dance floor angrily.

Sex Piston took a quick peek over her shoulder, but quickly looked away when she saw the grim determination on his face. Her stomach clenched in fear. Stud was no Ace; he was letting her know he wasn't retreating. He was merely waiting until she didn't have all her crew as protection.

She didn't need their protection; she was more than able to handle the horndog without their help. She would just stick to her plan to avoid him. It had worked for the last couple of months. Christmas had been dicey because her parents had invited him over to their house several times. Besides that time she had always managed to disappear when he had come over with his kids in tow.

She hadn't been able to resist buying his kids several toys for Christmas, managing to convince her mother to tell them she was the one to purchase them.

Her ma was still attempting to baby-sit, but Fat Louise had actually taken over the role until Sex Piston got off work in the afternoon. She had drawn closer to the older girls, unable to remain aloof, their attitudes not bothering her.

She was fully cognizant of the fact she had one weakness in her armor, and it was freaking kids. She loved kids. She loved the quick affection they bestowed, the curiosity in their eyes, and that they provided an outlet for her softer side, which she had buried deep.

Star was easily the most open of the three, but that was because she was so young. Meri and Keri were another matter. Meri and her had become bff's, but Keri was more quiet and sullen, disliking her. Although, Sex Piston noticed that Keri treated everyone that way, even her father.

Sex Piston actually liked the little girl thinking she was above average in her intelligence and her wit. She was able to give smartass come backs, which Sex Piston could appreciate. When she thought no one was looking, Sex Piston saw a deep sadness in her eyes, which had her wanting the girl to confide in her.

She squashed those warm and fuzzy feelings down, though, seeing the threatening glare from the girls' father from across the room.

"Let's go to my place," Killyama said.

"Sounds good," Sex Piston responded, taking Oz by the hand.

Her crew followed with their respective pickups.

Going out the door, Sex Piston felt Stud's anger as he realized Oz was leaving with her.

"He looks pissed," Crazy Bitch warned her friend.

"Good," Sex Piston said, unconcerned, as Oz's arm slid across her shoulders. Restraining herself from shrugging it away, she waited until the door closed behind them before doing just that.

Climbing into the passenger seat of the car, she was aware of the four bikers preparing to follow them back to Killyama's house. She leaned her head back against the headrest and then turned her head to look outside the car window, realizing for the first time she was getting tired of the partying, wanting to go home and go to bed instead. A sigh escaped her.

"What the fuck's wrong with you?" Killyama asked.

"Bored with these shitheads." She shrugged.

Crazy Bitch leaned up from the back seat. "Got something that will put your panties in a twist."

"What's that?" Sex Piston asked over her shoulder.

"I got us tickets to the races next month," Crazy Bitch bragged.

"Hell yeah." The women laughed in excitement.

The bike races only came once a year to the huge coliseum in Louisville. Each of them had their favorite riders and they would place bets with each other that their biker would win.

Life was suddenly lightened again as they began coming up with their bets. Laughter floated through the night as the green car drove toward Killyama's house.

Chapter Five

Sex Piston parked her bike as her ma pulled into the driveway behind her. Stud wasn't working until later today, so her ma had taken advantage of being kid free to run errands before they arrived.

"How was work today?" she asked as Sex Piston helped her grab groceries from the back seat.

"All right. Business is slow after the holidays until people get a couple of paydays to get caught up. It should start picking up again next month."

They packed the groceries into the kitchen and then started to put the groceries up until they heard voices coming from the back porch. Curious, they went to the sliding glass door and opened it, listening to Pops and Diamond talk.

Sex Piston had been furious with Diamond ever since she had found her and Knox together in Diamond's office. She hadn't been able to keep her mouth shut and had told Diamond everything Beth had told her about the MC Knox belonged to.

In her own way, she had been trying to protect her sister, but she could tell from her sister's face when she had informed her of how new women were initiated into The Last Riders that it had deeply hurt her. It had been the truth, but Sex Piston wished now that she hadn't been so harsh. There were easier ways to break that kind of information besides slapping her sister in the face with it.

"What's wrong?" Her father sat down beside Diamond on the swing.

"I love Knox. I love him so much." Diamond buried her face in her hands. "I don't even know why I love the big jerk." Her father put his arm around her shoulder. Diamond turned to him, crying on his shoulder.

"How does he feel?" Her father looked over his shoulder, seeing them standing silently behind the swing. He started to get up and let Ma handle the situation, but she shook her head.

"He doesn't love me back." Diamond cried harder.

"Are you sure?" Pops pulled her closer.

"Yes, now he won't even talk to me."

"Then make him," he said matter-of-factly.

"What?" Diamond looked up from his shoulder.

"Make him talk to you. It's what your mother did."

"When?"

Sex Piston knew. She had heard their voices arguing and had sat outside their bedroom door, listening, sick that they would break up like all her friends' parents had and she would never see him.

Pops took a deep breath. "When you girls were little, we broke up for a while. We argued over custody so we decided to live together until you girls were older. It was the worst six months of my life. I loved your mom, but she was sick of me putting the Destructors first. She didn't want me to leave the club, she just wanted equal time. I was stupid and put the club first and you guys second. When I missed Sex Piston's birthday party, she'd had it. Living with your mom and yet not being with her was terrible. I'm ashamed to say I did stupid shit that I regret, that I will always regret, Diamond."

Sex Piston remembered that time. She had tried to make everyone's life easier. That's when she had started cooking their meals, making sure to keep her mother occupied when she became bored or overwhelmed, and she never asked for another birthday party.

"How did you get back together?" Diamond asked.

"It was because of you, Diamond."

Her eyes widened in surprise. "Me?"

Sex Piston stiffened beside her ma at her pops words. After everything she had done, it was because of Diamond that they had stayed together?

"After you saw me at the club with that woman and didn't talk to me, your mom and I talked. She couldn't understand the change in you toward me. You went from being a daddy's girl to not wanting to sit at the dinner table with me, so yeah, she knew something was wrong."

"How did you know?"

"One of my men saw you running from the back of the club. When I got home I could tell from the way you treated me that you had seen. I didn't know what to say to you, and your mother finally made me tell her. It was the worst day of my life, confessing I had cheated on her and had been for a long time. The thing was, she had known all along and that was another reason she'd had a problem with the club. We talked all day and night, Diamond, and worked it all out, but I paid for that day for years. It destroyed my relationship with you and your mother wouldn't marry me for a long time. I had lost her trust; it took all these years to get it back, but I lost my little girl forever.

"Diamond, go after Knox, make him talk to you." Her father looked at her with watery eyes.

"But you loved mom, Knox doesn't even care about me."

"He ever give you a nickname? Even when you were messing around?" Her father turned red at his question.

"No."

"Not once?" he pressed.

"No, he always called me Diamond."

"Do you know why we called you Diamond?" her pops asked Diamond, his voice gruff.

"No."

"Because the second we saw you, we knew you were going to be the most precious thing in the world to us. Our precious jewel, our little Diamond."

Sex Piston was wondering why they couldn't have thought of something like that when they named her fucking Norma.

Diamond burst into tears, her arms going around her father, making Sex Piston feel guilty about being jealous over a name. Even though it was a freaking ugly name.

"If Knox hasn't called you anything else, then he knows what he's got, probably just too stubborn to admit it. Go talk to him, sweetheart."

"Maybe I'll go see him tomorrow," Diamond prevaricated, like she always did.

"Fuck that. Get off your ass, I'll take you." Diamond stood up, seeing her mother and sister behind the swing when Sex Piston couldn't stay silent any longer.

"Go ahead, Diamond. What have you got to lose?" her pops urged Diamond.

"My dignity?"

"Dignity isn't going to keep your ass warm tonight, move it." Sex Piston took Diamond's hand, dragging her inside the house. They were almost out the door when Sex Piston changed her mind and turned toward her bedroom.

"You can't go on a manhunt wearing that shit you got on." She went to her closet and pulled out a pair of jeans and jerked a top off the hanger. "Get dressed."

Diamond was wearing the dark blue suit she'd obviously been in all day, and for once, she agreed with her without an argument. Her sister put on the jeans and pulled on the top. Diamond's breasts were larger than hers and the top was low cut. The globes of her breasts were displayed to their best advantage.

"Do you have another top I could borrow? This one is too tight." Sex Piston watched Diamond look at herself in her mirror. The top looked great on her. Knox wasn't going to resist a woman who had tits like hers.

Sex Piston closed the closet door with a pair of high-heeled boots in her hand. She handed them to Diamond. "Put them on, and no I don't have a bigger top. That's the largest one I have," she lied.

Diamond sat down on the side of the bed, putting the boots on. When she was done Sex Piston pushed her down at her dressing table and took down her hair, styling the thick mass until it was curled and fluffy.

"Now you're done. Let's go."

"Sex Piston, I think I'm going to wait until I've thought this over a little more."

"Think over what?" Crazy Bitch asked, coming out of the kitchen with Killyama and T.A.

"Damn, I forgot we were supposed to watch Stud's kids tonight while they had their meeting," Sex Piston said, coming to a halt.

"Stud has kids?" Diamond asked.

"Yeah, three kids from hell. Is Fat Louise here?" Sex Piston asked, thinking fast, not wanting Diamond to volunteer to babysit anytime soon. Her movie choices would give the girls nightmares

"She's in the kitchen," Crazy Bitch answered.

"Fat Louise!" Sex Piston yelled. Fat Louise came out of the kitchen, eating a Pop Tart.

"You go on to the club and watch Stud's kids; we have somewhere we've got to go."

"I ain't watching those monsters by myself," Fat Louise argued back.

"If you do it, I'll take you out to dinner, anywhere you want to go."

"Anywhere?"

Sex Piston hesitated. "Yes."

"Even Popeye's?" Fat Louise's eyes lit up.

"Yes. We are going to The Last Riders' clubhouse to get Knox for Diamond."

"Why?" Fat Louise asked, confused. "We don't like that asshole."

"We don't, but Diamond's in love with the motherfucker, and what she wants, she's going to get," Sex Piston said resolutely. "Let's go; time's a-wastin'. It's Friday night at that club; things will be getting freaky there."

Diamond tried to interrupt Sex Piston, but Crazy Bitch dragged her to their car.

"My keys are in the house," Diamond said.

"They can stay there; we're taking my car." Killyama opened the back door and shoved Diamond into the back seat.

"Scoot your ass over," Killyama said, sliding in next to her.

Crazy Bitch got in the front seat with Sex Piston and T.A. grabbed the last seat, sliding in next to Diamond in the back.

Sex Piston put the car in gear, accelerating with a squeal of her tires. Driving like a bat out of hell, she drove toward Treepoint.

Diamond attempted to get Sex Piston to turn around, but her chicken-shit sister, for once, was going to face life head on, even if was a bald-headed bastard she personally couldn't stand.

"Fuck, no, we ain't turnin' around," Killyama said. "I've been dying to see one of their parties ever since Beth told us about them. Who knows, maybe we'll like them more than the Blue Horseman and we'll start hangin' with them instead."

Sex Piston grinned at Killyama in the rear view mirror. The Last Riders had no idea what was headed their way.

Chapter Six

The Last Riders' parking lot was filled with motorcycles and cars. It was the one day of the week that hanger-ons were allowed in the clubhouse. Diamond, Sex Piston and her crew got out of the car, staring up at the huge house. Music could be heard from where they were standing.

"Sex Piston, I've changed my mind."

She glanced at Diamond before walking over and taking her hand. "You can do this, Diamond. I'll be right there with you. I shouldn't have butted in when I saw him at your office. Now, get your ass up those steps," she said, giving Diamond a shove on her back.

"What if I see him with someone?"

"Beth caught Razer fucking Evie. She got over it." She shrugged.

When they walked up the steps, Diamond tried to hesitate at the door, but Killyama pushed her through. The sight that met Sex Piston's eyes was her worst fears confirmed about her sister being involved with Knox. The Last Riders were as Sex Piston had only imagined after Beth had told them of the wild parties.

Cash had Jewell on his lap, sucking her bare breast,

while another member had a woman pressed against the wall with her skirt up around her waist as he was fucking her. Razer and Beth were sitting on the couch, necking, and while they were the most circumspect of the group with their clothes still on, Sex Piston wasn't so sure what those two would have been doing if they had come in a few minutes later.

"Do you see him?" Sex Piston asked.

"No, he's not here."

"He must be in his room. Where is it?" Sex Piston asked.

"Upstairs."

T.A. put a hand on Diamond's back, pushing her toward the steps.

"Stop pushing me T.A.," Diamond hissed, her voice drawing everyone's attention. Beth's eyes widened and she jerked from Razer's arms before coming toward them.

"What are you doing here?" she asked as she drew close.

"Diamond is going to talk to Knox. He upstairs?" Sex Piston told Beth as if they stopped by for a visit regularly.

"I don't know. We just got here. Go outside and wait. I'll get Razer to go get him for you."

"We can get him ourselves." Sex Piston ignored her offer, taking Diamond's hand as she moved them toward the steps and then up them. As Beth followed behind, she saw Razer get up, coming after them.

"Sex Piston, I really don't think this is a good idea." Beth tried again to stop her. She ignored her, reaching the top of the steps before any of The Last Riders could stop them.

"Which one is it?" Sex Piston asked Diamond.

Sex Piston saw her take a step toward Knox's door. She was going to knock, but Sex Piston opened the door before she could. If the bastard was going to be unfaithful to her sister, she wanted her to know that shit right from the start. The light from the bathroom shined into the bedroom, highlighting the people on the bed. There were four people on there.

Diamond took one look and then turned around, running into her. She knew the instant she saw Diamond's face that she had made another mistake in making her confront Knox in his room.

"Mother Fucker," Sex Piston said angrily.

Diamond pushed through the group of women, her hand to her mouth. She got to the top of the steps before she stopped. Sex Piston, Killyama, Beth, Crazy Bitch and T.A. all came to a stop behind her as they saw Razer standing at the top of the steps, watching the women. She saw the sympathy in his eyes for Diamond.

"Bliss is mine," Diamond said, pissed off like Sex Piston had never seen her before. Sex Piston and her crew all gave a grin.

"Let's kick some ass." Sex Piston let Diamond take the lead. Her sister deserved first blood.

"What? Wait!" Beth yelled.

Diamond rushed back into the bedroom before Beth or Razer could react, burying her hand in Bliss's hair and jerking her off the cock she was riding. At the same time, Sex Piston went for Evie who was straddling Rider's lap, pulling her off backwards to land on the floor. Through all of this, Crazy Bitch held Beth and Razer back at the doorway, threatening them with a lamp she had quickly picked up from the dresser.

"What in the fuck?" a man growled, though Sex Piston didn't even pay attention to the male voice coming from the bed.

Bliss screamed, trying to get away, but Diamond had a good grip on her hair. Sex Piston was glad her sister had learned a thing or two from her. Evie was doing better defending herself against Sex Piston. She didn't like to brag, but she was the more experienced at fighting, while Evie was more used to fucking. As Rider tried to jerk her off Evie, Razer finally managed to get by Crazy Bitch.

Diamond threatened Razer as he approached her. "You get away or I'm going to smash your nuts."

No sooner had the words left her mouth than the doorway filled with Last Riders trying to get into the bedroom as someone hit the light switch.

"Diamond!" Knox yelled from the doorway. He stood there, dressed in jeans, a shirt and boots with his jacket on.

"What is going on in here?" Viper came to the doorway with no shoes or shirt on. The tribal tattoo he had on his arm and shoulder and the huge one he had on his chest had Sex Piston and her crew pausing to look at the biker, despite the turmoil going on in the room. Knox gave Diamond a threatening glare when he saw her eyes linger on Viper's display of muscular perfection a little longer than he deemed necessary. Hell, Sex Piston couldn't blame her sister. Viper made her own mouth drop open.

"I thought that Knox was in here." Evie and Sex Piston were still fighting despite Rider trying to separate them when Train got up from the bed, grabbing Sex Piston so that Rider could help Evie get to her feet. Sex Piston's hand reached behind her back and grabbed Train by his nuts. To Train's credit, he bellowed, but he didn't release her.

"Sex Piston, stop!" Viper yelled.

She let Train go reluctantly, who fell back onto the bed, holding himself. Sex Piston's top was torn and her hair was a mess from Evie using it to pull away when she had tried to strangle her.

"What are you doing here, Diamond?" Knox asked.

"I wanted to talk to you?" The statement came out too wimpy for Sex Piston's liking.

"Did you ever think of just calling me?" Knox asked, looking around at the pandemonium in the room.

Diamond looked confused. "I did, you never answered. Besides that, I texted and left messages."

Knox searched his pockets for his phone. "I've been out riding my bike all day then I went for a walk at Cash's homestead. I must have lost it."

"You weren't ignoring my call?" Diamond asked with a wavering voice.

"No," Knox answered, staring deeply into her eyes.

"You would have answered?"

"Yeah," Knox said softly.

Sex Piston watched as Diamond smiled and walked toward him, this time not looking worried about making a fool of herself. She walked up to him and circled his waist with her arms.

"I've missed you," Diamond confessed.

"I've missed you," Knox said.

Sex Piston wanted to vomit.

"Well, isn't that sweet," Killyama said in a sickeningly sugary voice. "Does that mean we can stay for the party?"

"No," everyone answered at once.

"We help you out and we can't even get a beer?" Crazy Bitch asked Diamond.

"One beer," Knox agreed reluctantly.

"Knox," Viper said in warning.

"One beer then they'll leave," Knox promised.

Sex Piston and her crew nodded their heads in agreement. As Knox and Diamond left the room with everyone following, Sex Piston couldn't help herself from watching Viper turning to go to a bedroom at the end of the hall where Winter stood in the doorway with a sheet covering her body. When she saw everyone's eyes on her, she shut the door just as Viper was about to enter. Unable to stop his momentum, he ran into the door.

Sex Piston snickered behind the badass biker's back as they reached the top of the steps and saw the front door open and Stud enter with several of the Blue Horseman coming in behind him.

Cash, who was at the bottom of the steps, turned toward the door. "What in the fuck do you think you're doing?" he asked Stud.

"We want our women."

"What women?" Cash asked, blocking Stud from coming any further into the clubhouse.

"Sex Piston, Crazy Bitch and T.A., you can keep Killyama," Stud said, looking up the steps. Catching sight of the women at the top of the steps with Rider and Train half naked sparked a fury within him that Sex Piston knew was a result of finding them in another motorcycle club.

"What in the hell are you doing here, Stud?" Sex Piston yelled, leaning over the railing. Her hair messed up and her top torn, she looked down at the President of the Blue Horseman.

"Which one touched you?" Stud yelled back.

"What?" Sex Piston asked in confusion.

"Which motherfucking asshole touched you? Because they're going to regret touching something that's mine."

"I'm not yours!" she yelled, putting her hands on her hips and glaring back.

"You damn sure are. Get your ass down here now!"

"We're not going anywhere; we're staying for a beer." Smugly, Sex Piston continued to ignore his order.

"Yeah?"

"Yeah!"

Stud signaled his men at her response. Knox didn't waste time, he moved Diamond back as Stud charged up the stairway after Sex Piston at the same time that the Blue Horsemen came through the doorway in a mass.

Sex Piston tried to take off running down the hallway, but ran into Viper who had come back down the hallway when he heard the new commotion.

"Just a minute," Viper said, preventing Sex Piston from getting away.

As Stud reached the top of the stairs, seeing Viper holding Sex Piston seemed to piss the biker off even more.

"Let her go, Viper."

"My pleasure." Viper let Sex Piston's arm go, and before Sex Piston could move, Stud had her.

"Let me go," she said, trying to twist free.

"Pike." Stud turned as another Blue Horseman came up the steps. "Take her to the truck." Sex Piston tried to struggle away, but found herself tossed over the big man's shoulder.

Stud turned back to the rest of Sex Piston's crew. She heard his smartass remark as she was carried out the door. "Now, you can go with her or be carried away, which is it going to be?"

Chapter Seven

"You son of a bitch let me go!" Sex Piston pounded on the truck window. Pike ignored her as he leaned on the door from the outside, preventing her from getting out. Bear leaned against the other door. Sex Piston knew it would be even more useless to try with that giant leaning against it.

"Fuck!" Sex Piston kicked the dashboard with the heel of her boot.

The truck door opened then and Stud slid into the seat. Putting the key in the ignition, he turned the truck on.

"Let me out!" Sex Piston screamed at him.

"No." Stud remained calm in the face of her fury, which pissed her off even more.

"How did you even know where we were?"

"Fat Louise."

Sex Piston should have known better than to trust her. She would cave the first time anyone questioned her about where they were.

"We were only helping Diamond out with Knox," Sex Piston explained, trying to calm herself down.

"I don't give a fuck why you were there. You've

belonged to the Destructors long enough to know that you don't go into another MC."

"To party. We went to help my sister. There is a difference. She's in love with the asshole," Sex Piston argued.

"What Diamond does is her own business. She doesn't belong to me, you do." His clenched jaw showed the fury he was trying to keep in check.

Sex Piston's mouth dropped open. "I don't belong to you. I'm not one of your bitches."

"Do you belong to the Destructors?" Stud questioned her loyalty.

Sex Piston snapped her mouth closed. The Destructors Club wasn't the same as when Skulls ran it, but she wasn't ready to walk away from it or her lifelong friends.

"Yes," Sex Piston admitted.

"Then you belong to me. Let's get something straight right now, Sex Piston. I've allowed you and your crew leeway because of your dad, but you keep getting in my face, disrespecting me in front of my brothers, I will cut you loose, regardless of my friendship with him. He wouldn't expect me to put up with the bullshit you have been throwing my way since I've taken over.

"I'm giving you warning. I've had enough and I'm not going to put up with it anymore." He had never used that tone of voice on her before. It was cold and harsh, leaving no doubt that he would follow through with his warning.

Sex Piston started to snap back at him, but she had to admit he had a point. She had challenged his authority since he had taken over and he couldn't lead the Destructors if he allowed himself to be constantly humiliated by the women. He had actually given them more of a chance than anyone else would have in the same situation.

"I'll cool it with the attitude at the club." Sex Piston turned away, looking out the window.

"That would be a help," Stud said, trying to keep the

amusement out of his voice.

Sex Piston cast him a sharp glance before looking away again as he no longer tried to hide his attraction to her. He was letting her know that he intended to have her when his gaze lowered to her top that had been ripped in her fight with Evie before catching her eyes with his. Sex Piston saw the steely determination that replaced the amusement on his face.

Wanting to tell him to go fuck himself, Sex Piston bit back the words as she tried to remain calm and get herself under control. Her temper had never been her strongest trait.

"I wanted to thank you for helping out with my kids." He changed the subject, loosening the sexual tension in the cab of the truck.

"I haven't done shit."

Stud cast her a curious look when she denied her involvement with his kids.

"It shouldn't be for much longer. As soon as the Destructors settle down, I'll leave Bear in charge then head back home."

Sex Piston felt a twist in her gut at his words. She wasn't about to admit she would miss his hellions.

"They have gotten attached to you," Stud probed.

Sex Piston remained quiet, not about to go there.

When he received no encouragement, Stud quit talking for the remainder of the ride.

Pulling up in front of her house, Sex Piston grabbed the handle of the truck door about to jump out of the truck.

"Sex Piston." She paused, looking back at him when she heard the serious tone in his voice. "Don't go near The Last Riders again."

She climbed out of the truck, slamming the truck door on his demand. She had no intention of going near The Last Riders again. She understood the warning in his voice that he was done giving her any more leeway. Trouble was going to lead to a confrontation she didn't want. She just had to make it until he returned home then her life would return to normal. Again, she ignored the gut twisting that thought brought forward.

She was becoming a sappy mess. Her bitches would make fun of her if they knew the thought of Stud and his kids leaving bothered her. Still, when she let herself into her parents' home and shut the door behind her, she couldn't resist looking out the side window, watching his truck pull out of the driveway and drive away.

* * *

"Watch that motherfucker ride." Killyama's voice could be heard over the roar of the crowd as they watched the motorcycles race over the indoor track.

Sex Piston knew which rider she was complimenting. He was a newcomer none of them had seen before at the races. His lean body controlled the bike at a speed that had put him in the lead from the beginning. None of the other riders could keep up with the skill he was showing, cutting through the bikers as they traveled the course.

A biker hit the wall of the course, wrecking his bike with a flare of sparks. The biker they were admiring dodged both the biker and his machine in a maneuver that should have had him joining the fallen biker on the pavement, but he held his machine steady in a show of skill that Sex Piston hadn't ever seen in all the times she had been going to the motorcycle races.

"I want me some of that," Crazy Bitch cooed.

"Me, too," Killyama said excitedly.

T.A. and Fat Louise were also hanging over the rails in the nosebleed section of the huge coliseum.

"Who is he? I haven't seen him at any of the races before." Sex Piston made no attempt to keep the admiration out of her voice.

"I don't know, but I plan to find out," Crazy Bitch yelled as the biker gained even more speed as two bikers tried to cut him off to slow him down. Making a move, he slid between the two bikers with barely room to spare.

"Damnnn," Sex Piston said, grabbing Crazy Bitch by the arm. All five women yelled when he won the race easily. None of them cared their favorites had lost.

"He kicked some ass with that race," Killyama said. "Why haven't we seen him race before? Think he's new?"

"Not riding the way he just did." Sex Piston raised on her tiptoes, trying to get a better view of the biker.

An older man sitting next to them butted into their conversation. "That's Wyatt Riggs. He quit racing about nine years ago. When I saw his name on the list of riders I couldn't believe it. He won the championship cup two years in a row. No one could touch him. He even competed in other countries and won."

"Why did he quit if he was such hot shit?" Killyama asked.

"No one knows. He just quit competing." The man shrugged.

A voice came over the loud speakers as the winners were announced.

"Let's go lower. I want to see what this dude looks like," Crazy Bitch said.

The women turned, heading down the steps and the exit from their area. It took them several minutes to get down to the lower floor where the guard blocked the entrance, but T.A. grabbed his attention while the others slid by him. They were still at the back of the crowd, but at least now the women had a view of what was going on; the huge monitors more easily seen, not the blur they were before.

"Next time we're getting better seats," Sex Piston muttered, frustrated they couldn't get any closer.

The riders were called to collect their trophies. The women ignored their previous favorites, waiting anxiously for Riggs's name to be called. Finally, his name was announced and the crowd went crazy.

Sex Piston's breath caught in her throat and she was

sure her eyes were deceiving her at the man who walked forward to claim his trophy. A woman wearing red booty shorts and a Harley t-shirt handed him his trophy then kissed him full on the mouth, treating the huge crowd to the voracious kiss.

"Is that who I think it is…?" Crazy Bitch asked.

"It can't be that fucking asshole. No way," Killyama said.

"It's Stud!" Fat Louise exclaimed.

Chapter Eight

Sex Piston couldn't believe that Stud was the man on the stage, who her and her crew had been cheering on minutes before.

"Why didn't he tell everyone he was a racer or that he was riding this weekend?" Fat Louise asked.

Watching the everlasting kiss on stage, Sex Piston started getting pissed, and she didn't know why.

"Probably afraid he would lose and didn't want to be embarrassed," Crazy Bitch said snidely.

"Don't think he was too worried about losing the way he can ride. I can't stand the fucker, but he can ride a bike," Killyama said with reluctant admiration in her voice.

"Let's go; I want to beat this crowd out of here." Sex Piston turned on her heel, intending to leave when she ran into a hard chest that was blocking her path.

"Enjoy the show?" Pike asked.

"I was," Sex Piston said, trying to go around the biker.

"Why don't you guys come with me and we can go congratulate Stud on his win?" Pike looked over Sex Piston's shoulder. She turned to see that Stud was trying to leave the stage, but several fans had stopped his progress.

"I think he's getting enough praise without us." Sex Piston jerked her head to the women and men trying to get closer.

"We can go backstage. I have a pass." Without waiting for her answer, he took her arm and led her through the crowd.

Sex Piston tried to jerk away, not wanting to see Stud. "Wait…"

Pike ignored her, propelling her through the crowd with a strength she couldn't get away from as much as she tried. Her crew followed, wide-eyed, trying to keep up with them despite the heavy crowd. Pike wound his way through the crowd before coming to a barrier where he flashed a pass and the guard stepped away, allowing them entrance.

He stopped the rest of her crew before they could pass. "Wait, he's not letting the others pass through."

Sex Piston tried harder to get away, but Pike kept her moving forward.

"I'll go back for them in a minute," he promised.

A corridor led to a room where several of the bikers were standing around talking to each other. Pike stopped when Stud saw them. Sex Piston watched Stud leave the biker he was chatting with, coming immediately toward her. She stopped struggling against Pike's hold, not wanting to embarrass herself in front of him.

"Enjoy the race, Sex Piston?" She felt his eyes slide over her body.

She was wearing a tight, black, leather jumpsuit with a silver zipper up the front which she had left unzipped to show the cleavage between her breasts, and black boots that came to her thighs. Her hair was fluffed out and curled. She had felt a lot of male eyes on her during the night, but none of them had aroused her to the extent that Stud's quick glance had evoked within her body.

"I've seen better," she lied.

She saw the happiness in his eyes. It was such a stark

contrast to the usual bored expression they held. Sex Piston didn't think there wasn't much in life that Stud hadn't experienced. The race must have given him the adrenaline rush that was missing from his life.

Sex Piston felt Pike move at her back.

"Tell her crew Sex Piston is riding home with me," Stud told Pike.

She turned to stop him, but he had disappeared in the milling crowd before she could.

"I didn't say that I would ride home with you," she tried to argue with Stud.

"I didn't ask." Taking her by the arm, he led her down the corridors until he came to a double door watched by a guard.

"Great race, Wyatt."

"Thanks."

Going through the metal doors, Sex Piston saw the crowd waiting. Women rushed forward, trying to get his autograph, and two security guards had to help them maneuver through the large crowd. Stud got on his bike, waiting for Sex Piston to get on. Reluctantly, with the crowd watching, she climbed on behind him before taking the helmet he held out for her. Stud then started the motor and pulled out slowly until he came to the road, merging into the busy Louisville traffic.

It was dark outside and the lights made the city beautiful. The bike took a turn and soon they were gaining speed on the interstate heading home. She was thankful the leather outfit she wore kept her warm; it was a three-hour drive home. When they stopped for gas, Stud had pulled out a leather jacket from his saddlebag for her to put on.

Sex Piston enjoyed the ride, confident in his abilities even before she had seen him race tonight.

They drove through a quiet Jamestown. Sex Piston's arms around his waist stiffened when he passed the turn off to her street. Stud kept driving, going down another street a couple miles away before turning into a driveway of an older home.

Cutting the motor, he got off the bike and then waited for her.

Sex Piston slowly got off the bike, calling herself every kind of an idiot as she followed him inside the darkened house.

"Where are your kids?"

"My aunt has them this weekend," Stud answered.

Sex Piston looked around the sparsely furnished home. It had a couch that looked new with a dining room table that also seemed as if it had just been purchased. Actually, staring around the small room, everything seemed as if it was brand new. The home was small, but was clean and organized.

Stud went into the other room as Sex Piston followed slowly behind him. He turned the light on in the kitchen and then moved toward the refrigerator.

"Hungry?"

"Yeah," she answered.

He pulled out a pack of hamburger meat before going to the cabinet and retrieving a frying pan. Sex Piston watched as he began preparing them a meal. While he fried the burgers, she went to the table and took a seat, enjoying the movements of his muscular body as he moved around the kitchen.

"How long have you been racing?" Sex Piston asked, no longer able to keep her curiosity at bay.

"Since I was fourteen. My dad raced bikes." He shrugged as he flipped the burgers. "I went to all his races. I began racing as soon as I was old enough."

"Does your dad still ride?"

"Not anymore." Stud handed her a plate with her burger. Going to the refrigerator, he grabbed her a bottle of water and a beer for himself.

"Why don't I get a beer?" Sex Piston asked, taking a bite of her burger.

"Because when I fuck you this time you're going to be sober," he said, looking her in the eyes.

Sex Piston almost choked on her food. Finally managing to swallow the bite of food, she took a drink of water while giving him a glare at the amusement he made no effort to hide.

"Very funny," she snapped.

"I wasn't joking," he said before taking another bite of his burger.

"It's not going to happen, Stud."

"Why not?"

She opened her mouth to answer him, but he raised his hand before she could say something hateful. "And don't lie and say you don't want to because I know you do."

"Dude, if your dick was as big as your ego, I'd fuck you. But since it's not, I think I'll pass." Sex Piston smirked at her answer.

Stud lips twitched. "My dick is big enough to satisfy you."

"Your dick gets too much action. I don't fuck someone doing other bitches and don't ever think that you can tell me what I want. Until you start wearing my panties, I think I'm the best judge of who I want to fuck."

Stud shrugged. "Fine. I won't fuck any other women. I'll let you have until we're done eating to make up your mind that you want to fuck me."

Sex Piston was almost speechless. Almost. "You're saying that you won't fuck anyone else while we're fuck buddies?"

He shook his head. "I don't need another fuck buddy. I can have as many of those as I want. I'm talking about something different, Sex Piston, and you know it. I like you, and I want to spend some time with you. I've been trying to do that for a while, but you keep running back and forth between Ace and any other asshole you can find to put up with your shit."

Sex Piston stiffened in her chair. "I don't fuck

assholes."

She could tell that he wasn't going to argue with her.

Sliding his chair back from the table, he took their empty plates to the sink before turning back to her. Leaning back against the counter, he crossed his arms across his chest. "Sex Piston, we could have a good thing if you gave it a chance."

Sex Piston stared back at Stud, confused as to what to do. Usually it was an easy decision. She had never really felt sexually attracted to any man, but she felt a spark of desire for him. She admitted to herself that seeing him race that bike had her body primed. In the few years he had been friends with her pops she hadn't really paid that much attention to Stud. She had been with Ace and busy building her clientele as a hairdresser. She had always noticed one thing about him that was a big negative for her, though.

"I don't think you can keep your dick in your pants any more than my pops or Ace could."

"I don't like being compared to other men, Sex Piston." Stud didn't take his eyes off her, which kept the desire coursing through her. It was beginning to scream at her to do him.

Steeling herself against her weak body, she managed to get her girly parts back under the control of her mind. She shrugged her shoulders. "You've been married twice, Stud. Your record with women speaks for itself."

"I married Reese. She followed me around the circuit and I didn't turn away what she was offering. When she got pregnant, I married her. We were married four years. I would still be married to her if she hadn't decided to fuck around on me with another rider at the club. They're together now and they care about each other. I wasn't going to stand in their way."

"I bet you didn't. Pops used to laugh about how you got your nickname when he thought I wasn't listening. You even managed to get another woman knocked up,"

Sex Piston said sarcastically.

"You think I'm stupid enough to get caught that way twice, Sex Piston?"

Sex Piston tried to understand what he was telling her. Stud wasn't a stupid man and it had surprised her he had been stupid enough to get two women pregnant.

He stared back at her, waiting for his subtle message to click.

"Star isn't yours?" Sex Piston could hardly believe the words coming out of her mouth. Star was a daddy's girl if she had ever seen one, and she should know—she had lived in Diamond's shadow with their father her whole life.

"This is just between us, Sex Piston, not your crew or anyone else's business. Candi, Star's mother, found out she was pregnant by Calder two days after he went into rehab. She was going to have an abortion without telling him. I told her if she married me, I would take care of the kid like it was mine. It would have killed him to find out what she was planning on doing. He's my brother, and I wasn't about to sit back and watch her destroy my niece. We got a divorce two days after she had Star.

"Are you going to tell him?"

"Maybe, if ever straightens his ass out. If not, no."

Sex Piston nodded her head in understanding. She had met Calder a couple of times. Stud's brother had accompanied him a couple of times when he had visited her father. He was younger than Stud and the more wild of the two. Physically, they resembled each other, but that was where the comparisons ended. Her father had told her that Stud was constantly having to get his brother out of some trouble.

"Candi has moved on to another club and she doesn't want to involve herself with Star. Every now and then she gets in the mood to play mommy for the weekend and I let her with supervision, but she doesn't get in the mood often," Stud said grimly.

Sex Piston had also met Candi. She was a bitch that

floated between motorcycle clubs, going from biker to biker. She was faithless and only had time for those who could supply her constant need for sex and drugs.

Sex Piston swallowed hard at the thought of never getting to know Star. She was a beautiful, little girl. Stud had made the right decision by stepping in and shouldering his brother's responsibilities.

Damn. She hated to admit she liked that he was responsible. He had not only accepted his brother's child as his own, but when her own father had asked for his help, he had, despite there being no benefit to his own club. The Destructors were mainly a group of bikers that had fallen into a rut, which was dangerous without the strength to back it up.

He was right; she was attracted to him. As much as she wanted to deny it, it was there. Damn, she was going to be weak-minded long enough to find out if he deserved that nickname of his.

Sex Piston got up from the table, going to stand in front of Stud. "If you fuck around on me, I'll walk away and not look back. After I kick your ass."

Stud's lips twitched. "Okay."

"I mean it, Stud," she warned.

"I know."

Sex Piston's arms circled his neck and then she did what she had been dying to do for weeks. She leaned in close, offering her mouth. When he lowered his own at her invitation, it was everything she could do to hold back the moan that rose at the pleasure that was better than she had imagined.

He took control of the kiss, showing her the benefits of giving in to him. His tongue surged into her mouth, exploring hers as if quenching a fire, as his hand went to her ass, pulling her closer. She felt his hardening cock against her flat stomach.

Stud lifted her up, packing her through the kitchen door and then through the living room.

Sex Piston's thoughts flew; asking herself if this was what she really wanted to do. Stud, whether he wanted to admit it or not, was like her dad and Ace. He might have his shit together a litter better, but not by much. He still lived the biker life and, while it was a big part of hers, she had learned that it was hard to make a relationship work with so many women attracted to the power of the position Stud held.

He opened a door in the small hallway before going inside and turning on the light. Sex Piston managed to tear her lips away long enough to glance around the small room. There was a big bed covered in a comforter that was soft against her as he laid her down on it and then following her down to lie on top of her.

His hands went to the zipper between her breasts. The black leather parted as he slid the zipper down, exposing her braless, rose-tipped breasts and her flat stomach. His hand went directly to her pussy, which was covered by the small lace panties she wore.

Sex Piston parted her legs further, giving him access to the flesh that was begging for his touch. She gave a small moan when his fingers found her wet opening before sliding forwards, finding her clit. Taking the tender bud between two fingers, he separated the delicate folds until he could expose the sensitive nerves underneath. His thumb began stroking her until she lifted her hips, wanting a firmer touch.

"Woman, I'm going to give you what you want, but you're not going to come before I can get my dick in you," Stud moaned against her neck.

"Then you better hurry," she threatened as his fingers went to the entrance of her pussy.

Sex Piston pressed against his chest until he fell backwards. Climbing off the bed, she peeled off her tight jumpsuit and black panties, exposing her bare pussy and the tiny butterfly tattoos on her side. She then climbed back on the bed, making sure she gave an extra wiggle of her ass before lying back down.

"You've got sixty seconds before I take matters into my own hands," Sex Piston teased, letting her hand fall to her pelvis, tracing imaginary circles on her skin as she waited on him.

"Damn it." Stud jerked up to his knees on the bed, unsnapping his jeans and pulling out his dick.

Sex Piston stared at his cock, surprised he hadn't laughed at her when she had insulted it earlier. "I'm sorry," she said as she watched him put on a condom he had removed from his back pocket.

Stud paused, staring down at her in confusion.

"For insulting your dick. It just might be as big as your ego," Sex Piston complimented.

Stud laughed as he lowered himself back down to her, his fingers brushing her wet heat as he fitted his cock against her opening. His hand then spread her thighs wider.

His mouth circled the tip of her nipple, drawing the rosy nub into his mouth as his hips plunged into her pussy. Her scream of pain had him jerking his head up as he saw a tear slide down her cheek. He didn't understand what his brain was trying to tell him. It was only when her hands pushed at his chest and she started struggling to get out from under him that it dawned on him what her problem was.

"You're a virgin?" Disbelief at what his dick and Sex Piston's reaction was telling him held him immobile.

"No... Yes... You fucking bastard, let me up." Sex Piston thrashed, trying to get away from the knifing pain between her thighs.

"Calm down," Stud snapped. "I'm pissed at myself for not preparing you better, regardless of you being a virgin or not." His hands framed her face before one went to her thick hair to hold her in place. Then, his lips came down on hers, gently teasing her lips apart.

His kiss soothed her hurt feelings as his chest lowered

to hers, surrounding her with his warmth as he pressed her firmly down into the mattress. He was trying to keep her thrashing body still before she caused herself more pain. Stud's hand went between their bodies, gliding over her clit, swirling the flesh until the desire returned hotter than before, before his cock slowly slid forward another inch.

"Do you want me to stop?"

Sex Piston felt the bite of pain she had experienced fade away at his ministrations. She felt his dick stretching her passage slowly as he glided deeper within her. "No, but you better not hurt me again," she demanded, hitting his shoulder.

Stud groaned as his mouth traced her delicate jawline. His groan echoed throughout Sex Piston's body as she felt him begin a gentle thrusting that enabled her to enjoy the feel of him inside her. Her breath hitched in her throat as he lifted her thigh to his hip and then moved slightly to his side.

She gave herself to him as she had never been able to do for anyone else. She felt his eyes on her as his cock slid in and out of her pussy. She could see the heat in his turbulent eyes before his mouth returned to the tip of her breast, gently laving it until it hardened into a tight nub.

"You're the sexiest virgin I've ever seen." Stud surged more forcefully inside her, increasing his speed as her hands moved to his shoulders, digging her nails unconsciously into his flesh.

His movements brought a tightening in her sheathe that had her tensing underneath him. As she came, his strokes shortened as his cock rubbed against her clit, intensifying her orgasm. He then thrust deeper within her, his muscled body shuddering as she felt his cock jerking its release. Her thighs hugged his hips tighter against her. It was the most erotic moment of her life as she lifted her hips, trying to catch that last spark of her own release.

Stud moved to her side before rising from the bed and going into the bathroom. Sex Piston waited until the door closed before she jumped from the bed. She used a discarded towel on the floor to wipe up the evidence or her lost virginity from between her legs before shimmying into her jumpsuit. She hurriedly zipped it up, ignoring the slight sting when she scratched her skin.

Jamming her feet into her boots, she then took off running to the bedroom door and was out in the hallway in no time. Reaching the front door, she flung it open when a hand slammed the door immediately shut and an arm wrapped around her waist, lifting her from her feet.

"I didn't think anything could send you running," Stud said mockingly.

Sex Piston thought about denying it, but being caught in the act prevented her from doing so. Instead, she tried to bluff it out.

"Fuck off."

"Now, is that any way to treat the man who you gave your virginity to?" Stud whispered against her neck.

"Would you rather I kick you in the nuts, which is what I'm going to do if you don't let me go?" Her booted feet kicked back against his bare shins.

Stud ignored the pain as he walked to the couch, sitting down with her on his lap. His hand went to her thighs, holding her in place, as his thumb smoothed over the scratch between her breasts.

"Talk," he ordered.

Sex Piston stubbornly kept her mouth shut.

"Sex Piston, one thing I know about you is that you have no problems speaking your mind, so I am sure you can manage to tell me how, with a body and name like yours, you managed to stay a virgin."

Sparks flew from her eyes at his words as laughter filled the air at her attitude. Understanding dawned in his eyes.

"You did exactly opposite what everyone expected of you, didn't you? Poor Ace." His laughter earned him a punch upside his head. He managed to grab her fist before she aimed for a second shot at his nose.

Frustrated at her inability to successfully hurt him, she let him have it with her words instead. "Fucking asshole. How was I still a virgin when we spent the night together? I may have been drunk, but you weren't. You lied to me."

"I did lie," he confessed with a boyish charm she didn't know he was capable of.

"No shit. Why?" Glaring at him, she unsuccessfully tried to punch him again.

"You're going to get mad."

"I'm already mad. I passed mad when you hurt me."

"I'm sorry." This time his thumb rubbed against her high cheekbone. He regretted being so rough with her, not knowing she was a virgin.

"So why did you lie?" Sex Piston refused to be charmed by the obviously experienced Stud.

"Several of the brothers want to get to know the women in your crew better—" he began to explain.

"You mean they want to fuck them," she corrected him.

"Yeah, well, that too, but those bitches won't make a move without your okay, so I figured that if you thought that we had fucked, you'd loosen your hold of them. You couldn't tell them *no* when you thought you had fucked me. You know, kind of like lead by example kind of thing."

Sex Piston just stared at him for his lame ass reasoning. She could tell that he was expecting another punch for his answer, but she didn't try to hit him. She was too hurt. She sucked in her breath, lowering her lashes so that he couldn't see the truth of her feelings.

"Well, it worked, didn't it? You should be happy with yourself. You and your buddies got what you wanted. Now, let me up. I'm going home." Sex Piston tried to get off his lap again.

"You're going to stay the night here then I'll take you home in the morning," Stud stated.

Sex Piston's lips tightened at the man who she had

mistakenly gone to bed with. Her temper let fly and she went nuts before he could react. Her hands went to his throat, gripping it tightly as her thumb pressed down on his windpipe. "Motherfucker, you used me being drunk so that you could manipulate me into doing what you wanted so that your lame ass brothers could get laid. Then you expect me to stay and let you fuck me over again? I wouldn't have fucked you tonight if I hadn't thought I already had. Why would I waste myself on you?"

Stud's hands came to her wrists, jerking her hands away before turning and lying her down on the couch and then raising her struggling hands over her head.

"There she is. The bitch couldn't resist coming out, could she, Sex Piston? I know it was a shitty thing to do, but I didn't do it for my brothers. I did it for myself. I didn't pour that Tequila down your throat, but I took fucking advantage of it. You've been keeping me at a distance for months, both as the president of the Destructors and as a man. You knew I was attracted to you, yet you weren't about to let me close. So, hell yes, I took advantage when I had the opportunity. I'd do it again." The charming womanizer was gone. In his place was a man determined to get what he wanted, despite the methods he had to use.

Sex Piston stopped struggling, reluctantly listening to his words. He was right; she had noticed his interest and ignored it, not wanting to get involved in another relationship that would lead nowhere.

She opened her mouth to let him have it again, but he forestalled her by taking her mouth in a storm of sensation that had her body rethinking about fucking him again.

His hand slid the zipper of her jumpsuit down to find the tip of her breast. He stroked the tip with his thumb while his mouth left hers to take it in his mouth.

Her hips arched as the ache of need returned. Her pussy clenched, wanting to be filled again. Sex Piston began to wonder that if sex the first time with him was so freaking good, just how good it would be the second time. Her body began to get even more excited at the thought of doing him again, despite him being a jerk. The son of a bitch knew how to fuck.

"We cool?"

Sex Piston refused to answer him.

His hand slid under the leather of her outfit, finding her pussy and plunging a finger inside her with no warning.

Damn. She felt herself weakening as he stroked her, the tender flesh stirring her passion higher, into a need that had her convincing herself that she could maintain a casual sexual relationship with him while she still searched for the man she wanted in her life.

"We cool?" he asked again, inserting another finger.

"Yeah," she lied, her body loosening, becoming more pliant under him.

She thought that she would let the bastard think he had won while she finally could enjoy a sexual relationship with someone she was actually attracted to.

She and Ace had played around for years, but her lack of sexual attraction to him had kept her from fucking him. She had satisfied him with her hands or mouth, but she hadn't given him her body.

The sad fact was, Ace had never stirred any passion in her body. That was why they would break up every few months. She would search for someone that didn't make her feel cold when they touched her and Ace would relieve the frustration he couldn't take any longer. They would return to each other when they couldn't find what they were searching for in someone else.

Sex Piston let Stud peel her out of the jumpsuit again, exposing her bared body as he lay her back down on the couch. His head went between her thighs where his tongue found her clit, stroking the sensitive bud before sucking it between his teeth. Sex Piston almost lurched from the couch, but his hand against her stomach pressed her back down.

The man had skill, and Sex Piston was woman enough to appreciate it as his fingers spread her wider. Two fingers filled her as he continued to play with her clit. She hadn't expected to be aroused as quickly when they had only fucked a short time ago.

"Your body is fucking beautiful," he said between gritted teeth. "Your tits are a man's wet dream and this pussy is tight as hell, begging me to fuck it."

Sex Piston held back her moan, still trying to hold a part of herself back. She couldn't stand bitches who screamed and acted like a cat in heat when they had sex, but damn if he wasn't working her sufficiently to lower her control to the point where her screaming would bring the cops.

Her hands went to his sandy blond hair, pressing him closer to her flesh that was begging for release. He gently bit down on her clit while his fingers spread inside of her, finding a spot that had her back coming off the couch again. She leaned over him as she came, unable to control her body's reaction.

Catching her breath took several minutes as he continued to stroke her until he felt her shudders stop.

Stud got to his feet before picking her up and packing her into the bedroom. Standing her on the floor by the bed, he spun her around until she had her back to him. He pushed her upper body down on the bed with her ass and pussy up in the air.

She heard his nightstand open and close and then the crinkle of a condom wrapper before his cock plunged into her in a series of strokes that had her flesh struggling to adjust to his size.

His hands rubbed her back as he started to fuck her, sliding his cock in and out. The sound of his flesh slapping into hers was an erotic sound that rose wanton feelings in her. His hands went to her ass, spreading the globes wide. She tried to jerk away when she felt his thumb against the rosette of her ass.

"Hell no," she said.

"Stay still."

He rolled his hips, taking longer strokes that had her hand grabbing the mattress to prevent herself from being pounded into the mattress. She felt his thumb begin to push inside her ass. A feeling of pure lust had her changing her mind about stopping him. Her climax struck when he buried his thumb to the hilt within her.

"You can't have an ass like yours and not expect me to play with it." His lips placed tiny kisses on her back, soothing her as he stroked his cock in her still tender pussy.

Sex Piston felt his chest shudder as he gave a hard lunge inside of her. Stud stayed immobile for several seconds before he stood up, removing his thumb and cock.

"I'll be right back." She heard him move away, going to the bathroom.

Sex Piston turned, managing to sit on the bed, her body trembling at the second climax that had struck when she had felt his. The man had her coming three times the first time she had sex. It was more than she expected the experience would bring. It was definitely more than Ace had been able to manage the whole time they were together.

When he came out of the bathroom, she stood up and went into the small room herself. Turning on the shower, she washed herself off before grabbing a towel and drying herself. Going back out into the bedroom, she saw that Stud was lying on the bed with his hands behind his head.

While she was still deciding about getting dressed, he took her hand and pulled her down on the bed beside him.

"Go to sleep," Stud said, turning on his side and pulling her close.

She had spent the night a few times with Ace, but inevitably she wouldn't be able to sleep next to him.

Thinking that she would lie there until he fell asleep then leave, she began feeling drowsy. Relaxing back unconsciously into him, she felt his thumb stroking the curve of her breast.

Clingy fucker couldn't lie still, she thought to herself before she fell asleep.

Chapter Nine

Sex Piston strummed her fingers on the steering wheel in the long line of cars, waiting to pick up Stud's kids after school. Usually, Fat Louise picked up his kids, but she had called to tell Sex Piston that she was stuck at the dentist's office. She would have asked one of her crew, but the beauty shop she owned was slow today, and Killyama and her were sitting around, bored.

They had gotten in the green car, expecting a quick pick up, however, it was taking a while and both women were becoming impatient.

"Where you been the last two weeks?" Killyama asked, bringing up the subject again for the hundredth time.

"Been busy." She gave the standard reply that she gave everyone.

"Doing what?" Killyama wouldn't drop the subject.

Sex Piston looked at the car in front of hers, not meeting her friend's sharp gaze. She had been spending the evenings at Stud's after his kids had gone to bed. She had also been avoiding the clubhouse, not wanting to see him with the usual skanks that hung around. Sex Piston hadn't let anyone know yet that her and Stud were seeing each other. She couldn't explain why, even when Stud had asked.

She kept expecting their time together to come to an end, either by him pissing her off or him getting bored with her. It hadn't happened yet and it was beginning to freak the crap out of her. The man never reacted the way she expected him to and he fucked better than he raced, which was even better in her way of thinking. It was becoming harder and harder to stay away from him until his girls went to sleep or he came home from the club.

He spent all his free time with the girls, only going to the club when they fell asleep and the sitter came in, which was only when he saw they were down for the night. She had come to respect the bastard for that detail; it was more than her pops had done for Diamond and her.

Every day, she swore she would break it off with him, yet find herself getting on her bike to go to his house, inevitably spending the night. She would sneak out in the morning before his girls got up for school.

"You fucking Stud?"

Sex Piston had never been able to hide anything from her shrewd friend. "Yeah," she admitted.

"He any good?" she asked with a smile.

"Yeah." She smiled back. She was relieved Killyama wasn't going to give her any shit.

"Damn."

Sex Piston laughed, but it was caught short when their eyes were caught by a large group of girls to the side of the school building. There was an obvious meaning to the circle of students—they were hiding what was happening inside the circle from the teacher's attention. The crowd parted briefly and Sex Piston recognized Keri as the one involved in fighting with another girl bigger than her.

"Killyama—" Before she could finish the sentence, Killyama was already getting out of the car and moving toward the girls. Meri was in the crowd, watching her sister. Sex Piston lips tightened at her actions, or lack thereof.

Finally, the slow line moved and she was able to inch forward. By the time she was at the head of the line, Killyama was waiting with the girls, giving the oblivious teacher a piece of her mind.

Keri and Meri climbed into the back seat, buckling their seatbelts quietly. Killyama got back in the front seat, slamming her car door.

"What was going on?" Sex Piston questioned Killyama while her eyes studied the girls' reactions in the rearview mirror.

"Nothing," both girls gave the same mutinous answer at the same time. Sex Piston pulled away from the school, turning in the direction of her home.

Silence filled the car as the girls stared out the window. Killyama threw her a glance, but Sex Piston shook her head.

When she pulled up to her house, the girls grabbed their backpacks and ran in while Sex Piston and Killyama were both slow to get out of the car.

"Did you find out the other girl's name?" Sex Piston asked as she shut her car door.

"Brittany Staff," Killyama answered grimly.

"She Allison's kid?" Sex Piston recognized the last name.

"Yes," Killyama confirmed.

The advantage to being the only hairdresser in town with any talent was that most of the rich bitches came to her shop. The very ones who had snubbed and made fun of her in high school clamored to make appointments with her.

When they got inside the house, Meri and Keri were already sitting at the table with their snack. Fat Louise was holding Star, watching with curious eyes as the girls remained silent. She turned to Sex Piston when she came into the kitchen.

She gave an imperceptible nod and then Fat Louise

took the little girl out of the room. Before she left, though, she started to open her mouth to question Sex Piston, but Sex Piston shook her head, motioning again for her to leave.

Fat Louise finally left, leaving the girls and her alone with Killyama who went to the fridge to grab herself a beer before sitting at the table. Sex Piston took a seat across from the girls, opening the bottle of water that Killyama had set down for her.

"Why did you get in a fight, Keri?" Sex Piston questioned the sullen girl.

"It's none of your business." Keri's smartass comment couldn't hide the hurt in her eyes. Sex Piston's eyes ran over the pretty girl.

Sighing, she leaned forward in her chair, her perfectly manicured red fingernail playing with the label on the water bottle. "When I was your age, I got in several fights at school—"

"Is this where you tell me it happened to you to make me feel better?" the girl said rudely.

"This is where I tell you to shut the fuck up and lose your attitude," Sex Piston returned her rudeness and one upped her.

The girls eyes almost bugged out of her head at her reply.

"I'm not able to make you feel better because you don't *want* to feel better. Right now, you're hurt and mad, but you're also afraid."

"I'm not scared," Keri boasted.

"Then you're stupid. You should be afraid. You should always be afraid when someone tries to hurt you."

Sex Piston's answer had the girl listening. Her attitude didn't change, but her curiosity was aroused.

"Being afraid makes you smart, keeps you on your toes. Not being scared makes you dumb, and you'll walk into their traps every fucking time." Sex Piston took a drink of her water. "But you don't want them to see that you're afraid because if they do, they will tear you apart like a shark sensing blood in the water."

The girls swallowed as Sex Piston talked.

"Who's the boy?" Sex Piston asked.

The girls looked at each other before Keri answered, "Isaac."

Sex Piston was willing to bet he was one of the kids in crowd.

Keri, being new to the school, would be considered an outsider, and her being pretty made the situation worse by arousing the other girls' jealousy.

"They call me names and tell me not to talk to him," Keri confessed.

Sex Piston nodded. "When I was in school, I matured faster than the other girls my age. I was wearing a bra when they were still playing with dolls. It made the girls hate me and the boys notice me. One in particular had all the girls crazy over him, but he would only talk to me, which pissed them off even more."

"What happened?" Keri asked while Meri listened with lowered eyes.

"They would gang up on me. I had my ass beaten a few times. After I let the boy walk me home from school, they started calling me *Sex Piston*."

"I thought the club gave you that nickname?"

Sex Piston gave Meri a wry smile at her comment. "No, those girls gave me that name to hurt me, to try to make me feel bad, which they almost succeeded in doing. Then two things happened to make everything I was going through easier."

"What?" Keri asked.

"My ma. They finally hurt me bad enough there was no way to keep it a secret anymore. I finally had to tell her what was happening and she laughed at the name the girls gave me. And you know, it was kinda weird, but when she and Pops started calling me Sex Piston, it took the power away from those girls who were using it to hurt me."

"What was the other thing?" Keri asked.

"Killyama, Crazy Bitch, T.A. and Fat Louise. Killyama were friends with them, and one afternoon they saw the girls going for me. They jumped in and helped me. They whipped those girls' asses. It was no longer just me against them, but *us* against them. There is always power in numbers. That's why the club your father is president over looks up to him because they know that while he is their leader he needs them also. A good leader is someone who uses the power of the members to work together to make what is wrong, right."

Meri's eyes watered and a blush filled her cheeks. "I'm sorry, Keri. I should have helped you."

"Yes, you should have," Killyama said. Sex Piston smiled at her friend.

"Even if you didn't want to get involved in the fight, you should have drawn the teacher's attention to what was going on," Sex Piston told Meri.

"I should have, but I was afraid that if I did, then they would start picking on me, too."

"They know that, too. That's why you work together to make those bitches leave you alone," Killyama said.

"We will." The sisters took each other's hands.

"Good. Now finish your snack. Your dad will be here any minute."

Sex Piston and Killyama got up from the table, going to the door.

"You know, Dad won't be happy that you're cussing in front of us," Keri said with a threatening gleam in her eye.

Sex Piston gave her a grin. "If you don't tell him I cussed in front of you, I won't tell that you almost got your ass whipped."

"Deal," Keri said, picking up her sandwich.

Chapter Ten

Stud stared out the window, watching as the sun began to break through the darkness of the night. He had come to dread the morning light as dawn approached. His eyes went to the bed where Sex Piston was lying on her stomach among the tumbled covers. The blanket barely covered the curve of her ass, making him want to return to the warm bed and wake her. The only reason he didn't was because he knew she would leave. She always left.

In sleep, the gentleness of her face was readily apparent, unmarred by the usual guarded expression she wore when she was awake. Dealing with Sex Piston was like trying to reach a rose among a garden of thorns. Every time he reached out to her, he was nicked by a thorn and would have to start over in a different direction to try to reach her. He was beginning to worry he never would.

His whole life, women had been easily attainable to him, yet Sex Piston remained just beyond his reach. He didn't know why she affected him the way she did, just that each and every time he had seen her the last few years he had seen something in her green eyes that had drawn him in and tugged at his world weary heart. She had gone passed his defenses, making him want the unattainable prize of her heart. If he hadn't tricked her into believing that he had fucked her when she was drunk, he knew without a doubt that he would never have gotten to first base with the woman.

Meri had broken down and told him about the fight at school where she hadn't come to her sister's defense, and about Sex Piston's talk with them. A reluctant grin tugged on his lips at her unorthodox talk with his daughters and what it had revealed about her own past. With Sex Piston's attitude, he would never have imagined that she would have been bullied in school. In fact, he would have assumed the reverse to be true.

His friendship with her parents became solidified at his discovery of their handling of the situation of Sex Piston's plight by giving her support and lightening a traumatic event with laughter. Those girls, who had given her the nickname, had sought to humiliate and instead, Sex Piston had turned it into a barrier against her and the world.

Stud remembered the dresses that Sex Piston and her sister had worn during their parents' wedding. Diamond's had been the sexier of the two, but Sex Piston's had been more refined and modest. Sizzle was keenly aware of the differences between her daughters, despite her seemingly haphazard way of raising them.

Stud turned back to the window, not for the first time, noticing that she had parked her bike in front of his truck to be hidden from anyone passing by his house. She kept their involvement a secret, not letting anyone know she had been in his bed the last couple of months. Each day, he saw the wariness in her eyes increase as if they were on borrowed time where they were concerned. She thought she would walk away from him if he made a mistake and proved whatever misconception she had going on in her head.

He moved from the window, sliding into the bed by her side as he lay down next to her fucking beautiful body.

His hand slid down her sleek back, curving over her ass as he slid the blanket away, leaving the luscious globes bare to his gaze.

"What time is it?" she asked groggily, not opening her eyes as she buried her head into the pillow.

"Almost six," he replied, his fingers sliding forward, finding her clit. He began to rub it until his fingers felt the wetness in response to his touch.

Yawning, she stretched and pushed her hips to his touch, her responsive body moving to deepen his touch. He gave her what she wanted, plunging a finger deep within her damp pussy. Her green eyes sleepily opened, desire apparent in their depths as her fingers grasped the pillow under her cheek, her need rising.

Sex Piston was like a cat; she loved to be petted and stroked. She responded to gentleness with a natural seductiveness that had his cock hardening and his balls tightening. He wanted to fuck her senseless, yet he restrained the wildness that was coursing through his bloodstream to dominant this woman and bring her to heel. Instead, he gave her another finger, driving her desire higher by stroking her inner walls in a movement that would heighten her sensitivity to his touch.

A small moan came from her lips just before she buried her face in the pillow beneath her. He removed his hand and, turning to his nightstand, grabbed a condom before ripping the package open and rolling the condom on his cock, barely managing to control the instinct to bury the naked length into her waiting pussy.

He knew she was on birth control, but she refused to let him fuck her bare, even after he had offered repeatedly to show he had a clear bill of health.

Condom in place, he slid his length between her legs. Burying his face in her neck, he took his time sliding his cock inside her slick warmth. Her back arched beneath him, pulling him deeper as he began thrusting inside her. His hands slid underneath her chest, seeking and finding her breasts. His fingers latched onto her nipples, gently rolling the tips until her felt the nubs harden.

She tried to spread her legs wider, but his thighs held her still, keeping her pussy tight. He stroked her harder as she began thrusting her ass back at him.

Another moan rose from the depths of the pillow.

"You're pussy is the best I've ever had," he murmured in her ear. She tensed underneath him and he began fucking her harder. "It's the last pussy I'm ever going to have." He felt her begin to struggle underneath him at his words, giving her exactly what she didn't want from him— a piece of his soul.

"While you're at work today, I want you to remember how it felt to have my cock in your pussy and my hands on your tits, and know that I'm the only one that's ever going to have you. Ever." His hands moved away from her breasts, sliding down her body, past her taut stomach, finding her clit and stroking it as his cock plunged faster inside her.

He felt the walls of her pussy clench as she came; his balls tightened until he couldn't control his own climax and then he pounded his orgasm out into her sweet as sin pussy.

She barely let him finish before she tried to throw him off her. "Get off, asshole." Romance was definitely not in the woman's arsenal.

Stud laughed as he moved to the side, letting her have the freedom she needed. She climbed out of bed as soon as she was freed, throwing him a stubborn look that let him know she was far from agreeing with him that he was going to be her one and only.

"Sex Piston, just once I wish you would let me finish coming before you're calling me an asshole," he mocked her as she scrambled into her clothes.

"Then don't piss me off," she retorted as she pulled her top over her tumbled curls. He wanted to drag her back into the bed and kiss her until the stubborn look disappeared, but knew she had to get to work and he had to get the girls ready for school.

Stud climbed out of bed and threw a grin in her direction. "How did I piss you off by telling you that you're never going to fuck another man?"

"Because I'll fuck anyone I want. You might have been my first, but you're sure as shit won't be my last." Pulling her boots on, she then grabbed her bike keys from the nightstand.

Zipping his jeans closed, he gave her a look that had her freezing in place. It was a look that left no doubt of his intentions, and gave her a warning that while he let her have her way with keeping their relationship a secret, it was only because he let her.

"Sex Piston, I'm going to give you a warning and you better listen up because I'm only going to give it once." Putting on his own boots, he faced the woman staring at him with an expression of stubbornness. "I'm not a man who is going to let you cut off his balls to keep you happy. There's room for only one man in this relationship and that's me." He raised his hand to stop her undoubtedly nasty response to his words. "I'm not Ace or those other fuckwads who have let you have your way to keep you happy. Try to make a move on another man and you'll see a whole other side of me."

"Whatcha going to do, Stud?" Sex Piston went to the bedroom door, her hand going to the doorknob.

"He won't be able to fuck you with every bone in his body broken, and you'll never doubt me again." His words rang in her mind as she left Stud standing with his hands on his hips, leaving do doubt in her mind that he meant exactly what he said.

The ruthless intent on his face reminded her of the night he had seen her in The Last Riders' clubhouse. No, Stud wouldn't like sharing. That was kind of a point in his favor. Nevertheless, the jerk would eventually screw up and then she would kick him to the curb. Of course she had to get tired of doing him first.

Going outside and getting on her bike, she maneuvered it onto the road, going home to get changed before work. She let herself quietly into the house, not wanting to wake her parents. However, as she closed the door, Skulls came out of the kitchen with a cup of coffee in his hand.

"Morning."

"Hey, Pops." Sex Piston felt the blood rush to her cheeks at his knowing look.

Rushing to her room, she took off her clothes and then took a quick shower. Getting dressed, she put on a red dress that clung to her figure, a pair of heels and her black, swing jacket.

Ready for work, she went out of her room to find Stud dropping off Star. Her pops was holding the wiggling toddler as Fat Louise came in the front door.

Star was fussy and she was fighting going to Fat Louise, squirming against Skulls hold. At Sex Piston's movement, the little girl's eyes lit on her.

"Sexy," she bellowed, reaching out.

Sex Piston thought seriously about walking by the child with everyone's surprised gaze on her. Yet, unable to resist, she reached for the little girl, feeling chubby arms circle her neck. A dollop of her drool landed on the front of her dress, leaving a damp mark, but she didn't notice it as she turned away, leaving startled gazes following her as she went into the kitchen.

Sitting the little girl in the highchair, she gave Star a cracker to tear apart as she began making her oatmeal. Fat Louise came into the kitchen, taking a seat and began playing with Star.

"I got offered a job at the hospital." Fat Louise had been out of work for the last year since her last job had ended with the business closing. "I can't turn it down, Sex Piston."

"I know." She poured the oatmeal into two bowls, setting them down at the table. She gave one to Fat Louise and blew on the other sticky mess for Star.

"I start Monday," Fat Louise continued, looking at her friend carefully as she blew on her own oatmeal.

"Okay," she said, feeding Star the spoonful of cooled oatmeal.

"What are we going to do?" Fat Louise asked.

"I don't know. I'll think of something," she answered, making her voice more confident than she sounded.

The kitchen door opened and her ma came in wearing her housecoat. "I'm sorry, girls. I overslept."

Sizzle went to the counter and poured herself a cup of coffee before taking a seat at the table. Sex Piston fed the child another cooled bite before sliding the bowl in front of her ma.

"I have to go or I'm going to be late." Taking a napkin, she cleaned Star's mouth and then leaned down to brush butterfly kisses on her soft cheek, producing giggles from the little girl that had Sex Piston smiling before leaving the room. Her smile disappeared when she went to the table to get her purse and saw that Stud was still there talking with Skulls.

"Later, Pops." Refusing to acknowledge the arrogant ass that was staring at her, she ignored the amusement in her pops eyes as he stared back and forth between the two.

"Later, Sex Piston," Skulls replied.

She had the door opened and had almost managed to make it out the door before Stud opened his mouth. "Sex Piston, you left your cell phone at my place this morning. Your dad put it in your purse so you wouldn't forget it again."

Slamming the door behind her, she almost turned back, wanting to wipe that smug expression from Stud's face, but dammit, she had dressed like a lady today and she was going to act like one, even if it fucking killed her.

* * *

Sex Piston motioned for Crazy Bitch to finish blowing out Mrs. Graver's hair as her next appointment walked in the door.

"Ready, Allison?"

"Yes." Allison Staff's narrowed gaze ran over Sex Piston's stylish red dress and heels as she followed her to the chair.

"What would you like done today?" Sex Piston was all professional as she consulted her nemesis from middle school.

"I need some highlights and a sexy style. Something that makes me look younger." She again gave Sex Piston's body a haughty perusal. "I have a date tonight," she said with a smirk.

"That's nice. Anyone I know?"

"I doubt it."

Crazy Bitch opened her mouth, but Sex Piston gave her a sharp look that silenced her friend. Allison wasn't acting any differently than she had acted since they had gone to school together. She had long ago learned to ignore the cruel jibes she sent her way.

Sex Piston ran her fingers through the woman's dull looking hair, which was in desperate need of highlights to hide the mouse brown color. Sex Piston walked in front of the chair and leaned back against her workstation.

"How's your daughter doing?"

Sex Piston's change of subject had an irritated frown appearing on Allison's overly made up face. She had wanted to brag about her upcoming date and then eventually drop the name of the man she was going out with tonight. Allison had always wanted attention, no matter how she accomplished her goal.

"Fine."

"I saw her the other day when I was picking up a friend's kids from school. She takes after you, Allison. She was trying to beat the shit out of a kid that's a couple of years younger than her."

Her hand waved airily. "Girls are always having disagreements with each other. You know that, Sex

Piston."

"Yes, I do. And I know that if Brittany takes after you, then she's a fucking bitch." Sex Piston dropped her polite tone.

Allison stiffened in her chair, glaring at Sex Piston. "If Brittany was fighting with someone, then I'm sure she had a good reason."

"I bet the reason has a dick that wouldn't give her the time of day."

Allison started to get out of the chair at Sex Piston's insult then stopped, sitting back down. "Sex Piston, I'll talk to her about her behavior. We were friends once, Norma. Maybe we could have lunch sometime, become friends again." Allison's sickeningly sweet voice was as fake as her tits.

"Allison, you can't fix what's already broken, you should know that. You were an ugly bitch when you were younger and you're still an ugly bitch. Now you need to get your ass out of my chair and get the hell out of my shop before I take my scissors to that straw you call hair."

"But I have a date tonight," she argued, unbelieving that Sex Piston was throwing her out, "with the football coach from Treepoint."

"Cut and Shop is up the block; I'm sure they have plenty of openings." Sex Piston picked up her scissors.

Allison paled as she rose from the chair, turning toward the door.

"And you better tell Brittany that if she so much as looks at Keri and Meri, me and my crew are going to pay you a visit at Boutique Bags."

Allison rushed to the door as Sex Piston took a step toward her with the scissors, brushing past Killyama, dressed in black leather. Allison gave a squeak of fear before rushing out of the salon.

Crazy Bitch started laughing at the woman as her car tore out of the parking lot.

"I take it you had a talk with her," Killyama said, going

to the soda machine. She reached under the flap, trying to snag herself a free drink after working the mechanism for a few minutes. With her orange soda in hand, she took a seat at one of the empty chairs.

Sex Piston nodded her head. "What are you doing here so early?"

Killyama shrugged. "I took a look in your appointment book to see *her* next appointment; thought I would have a talk with her. I should have known you would beat me to it," she said glumly before taking a drink of her soda.

Crazy Bitch finished Mrs. Graver, taking the cape off. Sex Piston walked her happy customer to the door after the woman gave her a generous tip.

"Sorry about the show," Sex Piston apologized, not really meaning it, but figured she better say something if she wanted to stay in business.

"Don't be. I enjoyed every minute of it," the older woman said in amusement. "See you next week." The door closed behind her, leaving Sex Piston with no doubts that she would recount the entire confrontation to the group of women she was meeting for lunch.

"You put the fear of God in her?" Killyama asked, using her foot to swing the revolving chair.

"No. I put the fear of my foot up her ass in her," Sex Piston responded. Her two friends laughed together.

Sex Piston felt the caring she had for her friends surround her in warmth. They had been friends since seventh grade and she shared a closer relationship with them than she did her own sister, Diamond.

She had changed a lot from that scared girl, but one thing she never took for granted was their friendship. No man could possibly be more loyal or protective of her than they were. Her mind shied away from the picture of Stud and his reminder to think about him today. No, Stud could never live up to the standard her crew had set, no man could.

Chapter Eleven

"Where's she at? I'm hungry," Fat Louise complained.

"Then order," Sex Piston told her, taking a drink of her ice water. Glancing at the clock on the wall, she saw that Beth was ten minutes late.

Just as she was about to give in to her own hunger and order, she saw Beth and Lily walk through the diner door, frustration evident on both of their faces.

"I'm sorry. It took longer finishing up with one of my patients." Her friend, who was exactly opposite of what someone would call a biker babe, was married to one of the members of The Last Riders' motorcycle club. They had met when she had gone to visit her sister at a college near Jamestown.

"No problem," she said, ignoring the tart looks from Killyama, Crazy Bitch and Fat Louise. T.A. had volunteered to give Fat Louise a break from Star so that she could join the girls for their monthly lunch.

The waitress, familiar with the group and seeing that everyone was there, came to take their orders. Beth blew her hair out of her face before finally relaxing back in her chair when she left.

"Why don't you come by the shop next week and I'll trim your hair for you?" Sex Piston offered.

"You know why. Razer doesn't trust you near me with scissors in your hand," Beth said with a grin.

Sex Piston couldn't blame the badass biker. Beth's hair was flaxen blond and smooth as silk. Her friend was beautiful and so was her sister, Lily, who was as dark as her sister was light, both in hair color and personality.

"So what have you been up to this week?" Beth asked.

"Nothing. Same old boring shit. Cuts and perms for the spring dance next week and everyone calling to make appointments ahead of time for prom. I always book up two months ahead," Sex Piston said, casually studying the two sisters.

"I bet since you're basically the best hairdresser in the state."

Sex Piston refused to let pride in Beth's compliment show on her face. Instead, she decided to be nosy and find out why Lily was looking depressed as if someone had hid her favorite vibrator.

"What's got your panties tied in a knot?" she asked Lily.

"I get out for summer in May and I'm tired of looking for a summer job. Beth and Razer refuse to let me work at the factory for extra money," Lily complained.

"Why not?" Sex Piston asked Beth.

Beth's husband's club owned a factory that produced and packaged survival equipment and supplies to disaster areas and doomsday preppers. It had been a lucrative business for the The Last Riders and Treepoint, the small town that it was located in, which was next to Jamestown.

"I don't know. Beth is constantly talking about them needing more factory workers to keep up with the demand," Lily said, casting her sister a pleading glance.

Beth didn't look back at her sister. Sex Piston noticed, feeling the strain between the two sisters, which was unusual as they were very close, unlike her and Diamond.

"I told you; it's not fair to take away a part time job from someone in the community that needs it. I can give you a raise in your allowance if you need it." Beth's compromise sounded good to Sex Piston. Free money always sounded better than working your ass off for nothing.

"I don't want you to keep handing me money when I'm more than able to work and earn it for myself. I have a job for spring break that starts next week, but it's only a short internship following a social worker for class credit. It doesn't pay anything, but I get credit towards work in my field of study," Lily explained.

"How much longer before you're out of school?" Crazy Bitch asked, taking her hamburger and fries from the waitress.

"Next year. I'm almost done. I actually get to graduate in December because I took so many internet classes over the last two summers," Lily said happily. "In the fall, I'll begin putting my applications in for a social worker in different states until I hopefully get a job. I want to work in Treepoint until I get a job out west. I have put my application in several cities in Arizona and Texas."

Sex Piston looked at her in surprise. "I wouldn't think that you would want to be that far away from your sister."

"Don't ask," Beth warned, taking a bite of her salad.

"Why?" Sex Piston asked anyway, seeing the amusement on Beth's face.

"I'm not embarrassed," Lily confided to the women at the table. "I want to meet some cowboys. Since they obviously are not going to be coming to Kentucky then I have to go to them."

Sex Piston and her crew just stared at Lily. If the girl wanted a cowboy, all she had to do was put a picture of herself on the internet and there would be a fucking stampede to Kentucky to meet the beautiful girl.

"I know a cowboy," Fat Louise said, a fry dripping ketchup poised in midair.

"No, you don't," Killyama argued.

"Yes, I do, and so do you," she corrected, popping the fry in her mouth.

"I would fucking know if we knew a cowboy," Killyama stated, looking at Fat Louise like she had lost her mind.

"Pike is from Arizona. He has a cowboy hat he wears sometimes and he has even done some rodeos. That makes him a cowboy, doesn't it?" Fat Louise asked, trying to steal a pickle off Crazy Bitch's plate, but receiving a smack on her hand instead.

"Yes, it does," Lily answered her. "Who's Pike?" She didn't even try to hide the eagerness in her voice.

Beth choked on her salad, and Killyama smacked her on her back several times until Beth managed to shift away. "Thanks, I'm fine now."

Sex Piston wondered at the wary look on Beth's face, but before she could question her, the diner door opened and Razer, Shade and Rider entered the restaurant.

Sex Piston watched as the hottie biker leaned down to kiss his wife in greeting.

"Got anything left?" he teased, looking down at her empty plate.

"No, you'll have to order your own." The men grabbed some chairs and pulled them up to the table, giving Crazy Bitch and Killyama's side of the table a wide berth.

Razer sat down next to his wife, placing his arm over the back of her chair. Shade maneuvered his chair between Beth and Lily's, and Rider sat down next to her.

Killyama looked unhappy with the seating arrangement. She took turns alternating between pursuing Shade and Rider. Both men, Sex Piston secretly believed, were afraid of her misunderstood friend.

"What you been up to, Shade?" Killyama's usually abrasive tone turned seductive.

He didn't take off his sunglasses, but his head turned in her direction. It was Saturday, and Sex Piston wondered if he was feeling the after affects of their Friday night fuckfest that The Last Riders participated in weekly if not nightly, from what Beth had confided when she had broke up with Razer before they had gotten married.

"Nothing much," he responded, ordering himself a coffee from the hovering waitress. Razer and Rider both ordered burgers and fries.

"Not hungry, Shade?" Sex Piston asked.

"No. I already ate," he said with an expression that dared her to question him further.

Beth and Crazy Bitch talked about her getting her GED and starting beauty school during the summer. Crazy Bitch had begun helping Sex Piston around her shop, discovering she liked working in a beauty shop. Sex Piston had offered her a job and had agreed to pay her tuition so that she could become a beautician.

"You going to let me do Beth's hair?" Crazy Bitch asked Razer.

"No." Razer didn't try to soften his answer. He was wearing a bandana on his own head of long, dark hair.

"I'll let you do mine," Lily offered, finishing her lunch.

"No." Shade's dark sunglasses landed on Lily.

Lily turned to Shade with a stubborn look on her face. "If I want her to do my hair, then she can do my hair. You don't tell me what to do."

"You still wanting that summer job?" he asked in a soft voice. Sex Piston watched as Lily's new found courage almost crumbled, but the girl didn't break.

"Yes." She stiffened in her chair, staring defiantly back at Shade.

"Then she doesn't touch your hair," Shade said. "It's fine the way it is," he supplied as an afterthought.

"She's going to need someone to practice on and I was thinking of getting it cut anyway." Damn, the meek woman had finally grown up and put her big girl panties on. Sex Piston was impressed; the heavily tatted biker was a hard ass.

"Then think again." Shade's hand went to hers on the table. Her delicate wrist wore no jewelry, but a red rubber band that the woman used to help with panic attacks. Placing his hand over her wrist, he turned more fully toward Lily, leaning into her space. He lifted his other hand to her black hair, twining a curl around his finger and pulling it taut.

"You want your hair cut? Don't you know that men like long hair, especially cowboys? I, on the other hand, think short hair is sexy."

Lily's body leaned as far away from Shade as she could without falling out of her chair.

Sex Piston decided it was time to step in before Beth and Lily both stroked out. Sex Piston had been around Lily very little, but she liked the young girl.

"I kind of agree with Shade," Sex Piston butted in. "Your hair is beautiful; leave it alone. It just needs a little trim. Stop by my shop during spring break and I'll trim it for you."

"Okay."

Sex Piston felt Shade's eyes on her as he released Lily's hair, letting it slide from between his fingertips. Lily's long hair suited her perfectly, surrounding her face in a dark, shiny mass, but she could trim it so that it had more of a style.

"I can give you a new look, but not have to cut much off the length." The girl needed to let Shade think he was getting his way while she still got what she wanted. Understanding dawned in Lily's eyes.

"Do you think that you could introduce me to Pike while I'm in Jamestown?"

Shade stiffened in his seat. "Who's Pike?" Shade's satisfied look disappeared at Lily's request.

"Someone that Sex Piston and Fat Louise know. They said he's from Arizona," Lily said, waiting for Sex Piston's answer.

Fat Louise started to answer, but Sex Piston cut her

off.

"I'm afraid you're going to have to wait until you move to Arizona to meet a cowboy, Lily. Pike has a girlfriend and I don't think she would appreciate me introducing him to you." Sex Piston tried to keep the worry out of her voice at the tension coming from Beth and The Last Riders.

Killyama straightened from her relaxed position, redirecting Shades attention to her. "When you going to give me a ride on that bike of yours, Shade?"

Shade's chair screeched as he slid it back from the table. "I'll wait for you outside, Razer."

Sex Piston watched as the furious biker left the restaurant after throwing a couple of bills down on the table.

"What ant crawled up his ass?" Crazy Bitch asked.

"Who gives a fuck? Rider, how about you?" Killyama asked, staring with grim intensity at the laid back biker. "I'll even return the favor and give you a ride on mine." The suggestive invitation left exactly what she was offering without question.

Rider looked like a deer caught in the headlights of a car. "I'm pretty busy at the factory."

"I'm available anytime. Give me a call." She leaned forward, her low-cut top showing the globes of her breasts.

"I think I'll wait outside with Shade," he said, hastily getting to his feet and also throwing down some money before hightailing it out of the restaurant.

All the women's eyes turned to Razer. "I think I'll head on back home." Leaving his half uneaten meal, it was obvious the cowards were beating a hasty retreat. Razer pulled out his wallet, handing Beth the money to pay for her and Lily's food.

"Don't you want to treat us to lunch, too, Razer?" Sex Piston taunted just to piss him off. Razer pulled out another twenty, giving his wife a kiss before his escape.

"Don't we get one of those, too, Razer? If you're not up to the job, send Rider or Shade back in," Crazy Bitch said.

Sex Piston had to put her hand over her mouth to keep from laughing at the look of horror that came over his face at Crazy Bitch's comment before he turned on his heel, leaving his wife with a gleam of retribution in his eyes.

"Wow, I wish I was you tonight, Beth," Killyama said, watching Razer's ass as he stormed away.

Beth laid her head down on the table and Lily buried her face in her hands.

"Did you see how fast those pussies ran? At least the Blue Horsemen and the Destructors stand their ground," Killyama said, picking up all the cash from the table and handing it to the waitress.

Beth and Lily just laughed louder.

Sex Piston and her crew had a free lunch. *No woman could ask for more,* she thought. She had a business she loved, a family that was healthy and best friends that could send some seriously dangerous men scrambling in fear.

Beth sighed. "I've got to go. I've got another patient to see before I can go home."

"That's cool," Sex Piston said as they all got to their feet. "Lily, don't forget to come by for that trim."

"I won't. Thanks, Sex Piston." Lily gave her a smile that had her pausing.

Taking her hand, Sex Piston gave it a squeeze. "If they don't give you a job at the factory, give me a call and you can work at my shop for the summer. Crazy Bitch will be too busy with school. You can replace her for the summer."

"I'll keep that in mind," she replied eagerly.

A worried frown marred Beth's forehead at her sister's answer. "We'll see what happens."

"Talk to you later, Beth," Sex Piston said as they went outside.

Beth grabbed her for a quick hug, giving each of her

crew one also. "Be careful riding home. That car looks like it's going to break down any minute."

"Shit, that car drives like a dream. Killyama keeps it in prime condition." Sex Piston ignored the insult to their shared possession.

Killyama ran her hand over the hood of the hideous green car.

"Some things deserve to be updated and your car is one of them." Beth's comment didn't faze Sex Piston. It was an ugly car, but it had character and it was big enough to hold all of them when they traveled together.

"It's a classic. It will last forever, you'll see. They don't make cars like this anymore."

Killyama and Crazy Bitch climbed in the back seat when Fat Louise grabbed the shotgun position in the front.

"Thank God for that," Beth said, waving goodbye as she climbed into her new model SUV.

Chapter Twelve

"What's wrong with Stud tonight?" Crazy Bitch asked.

Sex Piston turned her body, dancing so that her back was to Stud who was leaning against the bar, glaring a hole through her back.

"Don't know, don't care," she lied to her friend.

The first thing Stud had done when her and her crew had entered the Destructors' clubhouse was catch her alone when she came out of the bathroom to give her hell about The Last Riders joining them for lunch. She didn't question how he had known—Fat Louise and her big mouth. She was getting tired of her being Stud's snitch and she was going to give her hell when she had the chance.

"He looks pretty mad at you," Crazy Bitch said.

"I do not give a flying fuck." She enunciated each word.

Crazy Bitch's words were racketing up the seductiveness of her dancing, hoping to make the asshole miserable as he watched her move and not be able to touch her.

"Playing with fire, bitch," Killyama said from beside her.

Sex Piston shrugged. The music changed and she took off her leather jacket, exposing the flesh-colored halter-top, which showed the globes of her breasts. She caught several of the brothers eyeing her, watching to see if her breasts would spill out of her top.

"Shit," Killyama said, knowing her friend was determined to pick a fight.

Sex Piston grinned at her, but stopped when she saw her mouth tighten in anger.

"What?"

"Demie is all over him."

Sex Piston almost jerked around to see. Demie was the resident slut of the month. She had just started hanging out the last few months and was gaining in popularity by working her way through each of the brothers. They had nicknamed her Demie because she gave each man a demonstration of the skills her mouth was capable of. The men had even begun bragging about who had lasted the longest with her.

"What's she doing?" Sex Piston asked, already knowing what was going on behind her back.

"She's cuddled up next to Stud, rubbing his thigh," Killyama stated calmly, even though her hands were clenched into fists by her side. Killyama was the most protective of her and it would piss her off if Stud cheated on her, knowing they had a thing going on whether the club knew it or not.

Sex Piston casually turned her body so that she could face Stud and see what was going on behind her back. He was sitting on the bar stool, facing her with his eyes challenging. The fucker was giving her a silent ultimatum. Demie was standing between his thighs, her body, she sure, was rubbing up against his cock and the slut's hand was rubbing his thigh. Her stupid cow eyes were looking up at him, begging him to fuck her.

Sex Piston's hand clenched by her side. She never did well with ultimatums. Ace had pulled the same stunt on her numerous times, trying to get her to prove she cared. She never had. Not once. She was about to turn back around when Demie reached up and kissed Stud on the mouth.

"Hell no." Pure fury took over and Sex Piston lost the tenuous grip on her temper.

All her plans of showing Stud she didn't give a fuck went out the club door when she saw the slut's mouth on his. She walked across the room, coming up behind the tall blond who had twenty pounds on her. When she was within reach, her hand flew out and grabbed a handful of the blond bitch's hair, jerking her away from Stud.

Before the woman could do anything but reach up to her hair with a startled scream, Sex Piston planted her face against the bar. Not satisfied, she lifted her head slightly before banging it back down again.

"Do Not Ever Fucking Touch Him Again. If I see you even looking at him, I will beat the shit out of you." Sex Piston used the woman's hair to draw her from the bar, shoving her away from Stud.

The stunned blonde caught herself from falling by grabbing a table before righting herself. "You bitch," she screamed.

Sex Piston folded her arms across her chest. "That's right; I am. I'm *his* bitch." She nodded her head at Stud. "So that means you don't touch him. You can slut yourself out to any brother here and I won't open my mouth if they're dumb enough to fuck a slut like you, but you don't touch Stud again and you sure as shit don't put that nasty mouth of yours on him again."

Demie opened her mouth to say something, but her eyes slid sideways, noticing Killyama, Crazy Bitch, T.A. and Fat Louise all standing tense by Sex Piston's side. The light of battle went out of her eyes and a look of fear replaced it. Nodding her head, she slunk away as Sex Piston turned her fury on Stud.

"You want a piece of ass, it better be mine because if I

ever see another bitch up against you like that again, I'll fucking neuter you and you'll be the bitch in this relationship."

"Yeah?" Stud said, placing his beer bottle on the bar.

"Yeah!"

Stud got up from the bar stool in a movement that had Sex Piston blinking at the deceptively relaxed air he had portrayed. He had her around the waist and was leading her toward the back room before she knew what hit her. She tried to jerk away from him, but he just walked faster with her struggling against him. She saw him open the bedroom door that she knew had been given to him when he had become president.

He pulled her inside before slamming the door and pushing her up against it. His mouth slammed down on hers, showing her the lust that was fueling his body. His hands went to her hips, tugging up her tight skirt.

"Damn, Stud, slow down." Sex Piston tried to catch her breath, but he didn't make it easy. His tongue searched hers, twirling with hers in a kiss that was beginning to raise her own lust.

Reaching between her legs he touched her clit, which had her changing her mind about slowing him down. Wiggling her hips, she managed to put his fingers exactly where she wanted them. Stud moved his hand away and jerked at the tiny, black lace panties she was wearing, ripping at the sides until they fell to the floor.

Taking her waist in his hands, he lifted her against the door, holding her legs as they wrapped around his waist. Using his body to press her against the door, he unzipped his jeans and pulled out his dick. Then, he spread her wet flesh before putting the tip of his cock at her entrance, teasing her with the feel of him.

Her red hair brushed her face as her head fell to his shoulder. Trembling, her arms circled his neck as she surrendered to him without a word.

Slowly, he stroked his bare cock into her warm sheathe.

The pleasure of his bare cock inside her nearly drove her into a climax, but Sex Piston gritted her teeth as she tried to hold on to the pleasure as long as she could manage. Her hips began pushing down as he stroked upwards, sending his cock sliding deep within her clenching pussy.

Her mouth went to his throat, kissing and licking the salty taste of his skin. She sucked a small piece of his flesh into her mouth as he moved within her. Her moans muffled by his skin.

Stud began moving harder inside her, slamming her against the door as he increased the speed of his thrusts. One hand went to her ass, sliding between the globes to find the tiny rosette he was searching for. Without any warning, he thrust a long finger inside, breaching the tiny hole.

Lacking any coherent thoughts, Sex Piston bit down on the flesh in her mouth, her hands clenching onto his shoulders as her orgasm hit her with a wave of desire that couldn't be held back any longer.

"Fuck," Stud groaned, pressing her flat against the door as his cock jerked his own climax into her slippery pussy.

When she finished trembling, she raised her head. Stud let her legs slip down from his waist, setting her back down on the floor.

Sex Piston slid her skirt back down her hips, not looking at Stud as he took her hand and led her into the bathroom. Taking a wash cloth, he soaped and wetted it and then sat her on the counter before he went down on his knees.

"Spread your legs."

Sex Piston widened her stance, letting him wash her as she looked down at him. She started to reach out and touch his hair, wanting something she wasn't willing to recognize, when her eyes caught the mark on the side of his neck.

"Shit."

"What?" he asked, throwing the wet cloth into a

basket in the corner and then going to the sink to wash his own hands. Zipping and snapping his jeans, he looked at her curiously.

"Your neck." Sex Piston's hand went to her mouth.

Stud turned back to the mirror. Sex Piston watched as he took in the mark she had left behind.

"I don't think you left any doubt in anyone's mind that you're my old lady, do you?"

Sex Piston's lips tightened at his remark. Jumping down from the counter, she stormed out of the bathroom, stopping in front of the closed bedroom door. She reached down to pick up her torn underwear before going to the trashcan by the bed and throwing them away. All the while she avoided his eyes as he came out of the bathroom.

"Is it so bad that everyone knows?"

"I've played this game before, Stud," Sex Piston said. "I didn't want to play it again."

"I'm not playing you, Sex Piston." His hard voice drew her reluctant gaze. "It's not about the pussy, is it, Sex Piston? You're fucking beautiful. You have a body that's hot as hell and you know it because you work it with those clothes you wear. You're not worried about me fucking another bitch. You want me to want you. What you don't want is to want me back. Isn't that right, Sex Piston? You're letting me in enough to have that body, which is more than you gave Ace, but you're still trying to keep me out like you keep everyone out, except your crew."

Sex Piston lowered her lashes, trying to hide the panic coursing through her veins. She took a step toward the door, but Stud moved to block her path.

"You don't have to protect yourself from me, Sex Piston. I've never let anyone down my whole life." He reached out to touch her cheek, but she jerked her head back.

"What do you want from me, Stud?" Frustrated, she waved her hand toward the door. "Everyone out there knows we're hooked up now."

"I want you to admit this is more than fucking," Stud responded.

"It's all about the fucking," she shot back stubbornly.

Stud shook his head. "No, it's not, and you know it. You're smart enough to know I care about you, but you won't admit the same."

She refused to respond to his misconception. She didn't care about him. Her traitorous body wanted him, but that was all there was to it. Once she had enough of his dick then she'd move on to the next one.

"You can lie to yourself all you want, Sex Piston, but I know that you care about me."

Stud's stubbornness was beginning to get to her. "You're full of shit!"

She had to get out of the close confines of the room, away from his searching eyes that were trying to find emotions that she had buried years ago when she realized how people could suck you dry and leave you with nothing left to give.

"No, I'm not. You've reorganized your whole life around my kids. You added them into the group of people you take care of."

Sex Piston tensed.

"You take care of your mom, cooking and cleaning because she's ditzy as fuck. You see that your dad takes all his medicine when he's supposed to and eats right so that his diabetes stays under control. That's why you don't have your own place because you've been taking care of them for a long time. I'm willing to bet that you took care of Diamond before she took off for college."

Sex Piston's bottom lip trembled. She bit down on it to stop the betraying movement.

"You gave Crazy Bitch a job and are planning on taking care of her tuition. You promised one of your clients free services at your shop for a year if she helped get Fat Louise a job at the hospital. T.A.'s ex-boyfriend got violent with her a couple months back; you bought her a gun and made her take self defense lessons, and moved Killyama in with her. The only one I can tell that you haven't had to shoulder is Killyama, and that bitch would fucking die for you."

He took a step closer to her. Sex Piston warily stood her ground as he moved closer, feeling his arms close around her. "I appreciate the help with the girls, but my aunt has been doing it for years and she is missing them. She lives with me and I haven't moved her here because I had every intention of you being in my bed at night. So Fat Louise can start her job Monday without you worrying about the girls. The club will pitch in and pay for Crazy Bitch's beauty school. Me and the brothers already handled T.A.'s ex. You were right by the way; he's a mean motherfucker. I've got Popcorn watching him now.

"Caring about me won't make you weak, Sex Piston. You've been fighting against the world for so long that you haven't seen that the war's over. Your bullies are gone, and there's not a person whose ass you can't kick."

"I don't need your help."

"I know you don't need anyone, Sex Piston, but I do want you to need me in your life. I need you because I need your sexy body in my bed, your sassy mouth giving me hell and the way you look at me when you think no one is looking."

Sex Piston saw a flash of vulnerability cross his face before he smoothed out his expression. Taking a step back from her, he let her have her space back.

"I'll think about it," Sex Piston said stubbornly.

"You do that." His lips twitched in amusement.

Sex Piston smoothed her leather skirt down over her hips then smoothed down her tumbled hair before adjusting her breasts in the halter-top. When she was finished, she went to the door. Her hand was on the doorknob when Stud stopped her again.

"Sex Piston?"

"What?!" She turned back around.

"Come here."

She started to ignore him, but for some inexplicable reason she found herself going back to him. He pulled her toward him when she was within reach, giving her a sweet kiss that tugged at her heartstrings. He then released her with a pat on the ass.

"Now you can go."

She turned on her heel, leaving him in the bedroom, not even slamming the door behind her at his arrogant attitude. The kiss had been that good. He deserved a reward.

To soothe her bitchy side, she told herself that next time, she'd make him eat his nuts if he got mushy with her again.

Chapter Thirteen

"How much longer you going to be?" Fat Louise complained.

"Give me five minutes," Sex Piston snapped at her friend, giving a final touch to the hairstyle she had been working on for the last twenty minutes.

"All done, Susan," she said, removing the black cape draped across the woman.

"Thanks, Sex Piston. See you next month."

"I'll mark you in. Thanks, Susan," she said with a smile, placing the cape in a basket to be washed.

"Bye." Susan waved at the women sitting around the shop, who were waiting for Sex Piston to get off.

"Finally, I thought you'd never get finished," T.A. said, slapping the magazine down on the table.

Crazy Bitch, Killyama, T.A. and Fat Louise were all waiting for her to finish so they could take Fat Louise out for dinner to celebrate her first week at work.

"It's not like Popeye's is going to close anytime soon," Sex Piston said, getting the broom out of the closet and going to sweep up the hair on the floor left behind after Susan's cut.

"I'm starving. I haven't eaten since lunch."

"You've been snacking on chips and soda; there is no way you are hungry," Crazy Bitch remarked, rolling her eyes at Fat Louise.

The door opening drew Sex Piston's attention away from her arguing friends. She was surprised when Lily walked in the door.

"Your appointment isn't until tomorrow," was all she could think to say.

Lily grinned at her. "I know. I was nearby, visiting a home with the social worker I was shadowing for my internship. Traffic is at a standstill to Treepoint, so I'm caught in town until it clears. Beth suggested I hang out here with you guys until the road is clear, if that's okay with you guys?"

"That's cool," Sex Piston said softly. With Lily, for some inexplicable reason, she and her crew always toned down their natural abrasiveness.

"We heard the sirens." Crazy Bitch closed the cash register, placing the night's deposit in Sex Piston's purse. "I wondered why there wasn't much traffic outside."

"There is a big fire at a house. They're having trouble getting it out. The radio said that several fire departments from three different counties are there. Police are redirecting traffic to the interstate, but there is no way to go around any of the other counties," Lily explained.

"I wonder whose place could have caught on fire that needed that many fire trucks," Killyama said, taking out her cell phone.

"It began at a house next to the railroad tracks," Lily explained. "If I hadn't stopped for coffee with my mentor, I would have been home before the fire started."

Killyama whistled, setting her cell phone down on the counter. "That's Cracker's place; he's the resident hoarder. I bet he has three piles of tires in his backyard. The city has been trying to get him to clean his junk for years. The lumber yard is right behind it. If it spreads, it's going to take more than three trucks to put that fire out."

"That should keep our only two cops thrilled. The most they get to do is nab an occasional shoplifter around here," T.A. remarked. "Anything worse, they call the state police and it takes them a good twenty minutes to get here from Treepoint."

"Since we're stuck here, let's go ahead and get your hair done."

Sex Piston hoped Cracker and his dogs were all right. He would often come by the club for a beer. He didn't belong to the club, but no one had the heart to throw him out.

"Sounds good," Lily agreed.

Lily took a seat at her station while Sex Piston put the broom back in the closet. Putting a cape around Lily, she took a minute to study the beautiful girl. Her hair lay silky against her back.

"Going to let me work my magic?" Sex Piston asked, studying the girl's reaction closely.

"Go for it. I'm ready for a change. I think short hair is cute," she said, then added, "Just not too short. About half of what it is now."

Sex Piston asked herself whose reaction she was worried about most; if cowboys really liked longer hair or Shade saying that he liked short hair.

"I don't think Shade is ready for your hair to be cut short," Sex Piston probed.

"He's just overprotective because Razer and him are best friends. He sees me as a little sister, like Razer does."

Sex Piston looked deep into her eyes to find that she really believed the shit she was saying.

Sex Piston's gaze paused briefly over Lily's hair. The girl was too innocent for her own good. She had seen something else in Lily's eyes that hurt Sex Piston deep inside her heart, but she didn't know why.

Her lips tightened. A heads up wouldn't hurt.

Sex Piston got to work on Lily's hair by first taking her

to the sink and efficiently washing it. When she was finished, she wrapped her head in a clean towel then put her back in the chair in front of her station. Her foot pumped the chair to the height she needed before she combed Lily's hair out and then began.

"He call you *little sis* like Razer does?" she asked, grabbing her scissors to begin cutting.

"No."

Killyama came around to lean against the workstation as the others unobtrusively moved closer to listen. Fat Louise put her bag of chips down and moved to one on the chairs closer to Lily. Crazy Bitch sat down in the chair next to Lily's, using her foot to move the chair in circles as she listened. T.A. began sweeping, but didn't get past where Crazy Bitch was sitting.

"You think of him like Razer, a big brother?" Sex Piston took a step back, looked at Lily's hair for a second and then resumed cutting.

"Of course. He's more overbearing than Razer, but I figure he's just been lonely since Beth and Razer have married. I'm sure Shade and Razer don't get to spend as much time hanging out together anymore."

"I know for a fact they don't spend as much time together since Beth," Sex Piston said wryly. Beth had told her why she had broken up with Razer when they had first started dating. The men shared women and Beth had caught them in the act. Beth sure as fuck wouldn't have told her innocent sister that piece of news.

Shade had drawn her and her friends' attention since the first time they had seen him at the Pink Slipper, covered in tats. His badass biker vibe had everyone, including herself—she wasn't ashamed to admit wanting a piece of the gorgeous man—wanting him.

Personally, Sex Piston knew a man as dominant as Shade would never be attracted to women with aggressive dominant personalities like her and her friends. Lily, on the other hand, would be a perfect submissive for the man and she was willing to bet he fucking knew it.

Being a friend of Razer's wouldn't protect her for much longer. That thin line was wearing down. She had noticed that in the diner when he had little patience with having no control over whether or not Lily cut her hair.

"He's more than overbearing; he's a Dom." Sex Piston's scissors kept cutting, letting Killyama take over Lily's education—something Beth should have already done, but Sex Piston doubted she knew about that kinky shit.

"A Dom?" Lily's eyes widened in the mirror, staring at Killyama.

"Don't you read books? Haven't you heard of Fifty-One Shades of Black and Blue?" Killyama wisecracked.

It was everything Sex Piston could do to hold her scissors steady, desperately biting down on her tongue to keep from adding a raunchy comeback.

"I've heard of books like that, but I've never read them," Lily said, her head lowered to her lap.

"What's your email? I'll lend you a few copies," Killyama said, then added beneath her breath, "You're going to need them."

"No thanks. I don't have time for extra reading right now. I have finals coming up. Besides that, I really only read inspirational books."

"They inspired me," Killyama said with a big smile.

"Can I borrow them?" Fat Louise asked.

"No," Killyama, Crazy Bitch, T.A. and Sex Piston all spoke at the same time.

"Send them to me. I need some fresh ideas," Crazy Bitch said, still swinging the chair back and forth. "I have a new whip to break in."

When Lily began staring at Crazy Bitch with fear, which Sex Piston had to admit she kinda had her reconsidering their friendship, she changed the conversation to Lily's friend.

"What's your roommate, Penni, doing for spring

break?"

"She's doing an internship, too. She wants to get a job with them when she graduates in May." Lily didn't look happy that her friend would be graduating before her. "I'm going to miss having her as a roommate."

Sex Piston took her time styling Lily's hair. It was beginning to get dark when Lily had arrived and now it was completely dark outside.

Out of the corner of her eye she saw Killyama go to the door and look out.

Finished, Sex Piston took a step back, admiring her work. The result was stunning.

"Holy shit," the women surrounding Lily exclaimed.

The young girl had been transformed into a sexy woman. Her hair had been layered to let the dark locks frame her face, drawing attention to her beautiful eyes and full lips. The length remained almost the same, yet it appeared fuller and thicker with the addition of the layers Sex Piston had cut.

Sex Piston watched as Lily stared at her image in the mirror. She could tell that Lily was uncomfortable with the look. "If you don't like it, all you have to do is blow dry it straight when you wash it," she said gently, laying her hand on her arm underneath the cape. "If you give it a couple of days, you'll get used to it. The style is a more mature look for you."

"It sure as hell is. If I was a guy, I'd do you. Hell, I love dick, but you're making me consider switching, Lily," T.A. joked, touching Lily's other arm.

Sex Piston could tell the smile Lily gave her was forced.

"It's nice. I was just expecting you to cut it shorter." Her murmur was low and filled with disappointment.

"Lily, short hair isn't going to make you less hot." Lily shot a surprised look at Sex Piston's intuitive comment. "Sometimes, the only way to fight what you're afraid of is to be a better fighter. A girl can always be overwhelmed, but a woman knows how to overwhelm a man," Sex

Piston replied with the best advice she could.

Lily nodded, seeming to straighten in her seat as she gingerly touched her new hairstyle.

Sex Piston noticed Killyama motioning to her.

"I'll be right back." Leaving Lily's side with the other women remarking on her new style, she went to stand next to Killyama who she had noticed had gone out back and then had returned with a worried look.

"What's up?" she asked. Nothing scared Killyama, so to see her worried, sent alarm signals running down her back.

"Someone's messed with the parking lot lights. It's dark as shit out there and the other shops next to you are already closed."

"Maybe it's just the timer malfunctioning?" Sex Piston tried to think of a reason that the reliable system that automatically turned the lights on when it became dark had failed.

"I don't think so. I think we should call the club and ask a few of the brothers to escort us out of here. I checked the back door; it's locked. Let's lock the front door and stay put until they get here."

"You sure? They'll give us hell if we drag their asses out for nothing."

"Ace may have, but Stud wouldn't. I don't like the feel of this, Sex Piston. T.A. and I both left our weapons in the trunk of the car because of all the kids you have running around in here when their moms are getting their hair cut."

"Call them. I'll lock the door." If Killyama felt threatened, then they needed to worry. Sex Piston trusted her instincts.

Moving toward the door, she stopped at the sight of a man walking in the door with a gun in his hand.

"Dale, what are you doing!?" T.A. took a step forward, but Crazy Bitch took her arm and pulled her back.

"What do you think, you stupid bitch? I told you that I wasn't done with you. Did you think that biker watching me was going to protect you? Hell, Killyama was better. The one that you sent to replace her won't be watching anyone anymore." He smirked.

The door opened again and Joker came in. Momentarily, relief flew through Sex Piston until shock replaced it when she saw the gun in his hand before he turned and locked the door.

"Get them in the back so no one can see them through the windows," Joker ordered.

"Who's going to see them?" Dale snickered, but motioned for the women to move toward the back of the shop.

"Traffic may be getting slowly through, but we lost too much time waiting to see if someone was going to come in behind her." Joker nodded his head toward a pale Lily who hadn't turned her chair around to face the men. Instead, she was watching them through the mirror with terror-filled eyes.

"Move it!" Dale ordered.

Killyama took a threatening step toward the men until Joker pointed his gun at her.

"Take another step toward me, you psycho bitch, and I will shoot one of them and Dale will kill you. Now move that ass of yours."

Killyama froze before turning and walking toward the back of the shop.

Sex Piston, Crazy Bitch, T.A. and Fat Louise started to follow Killyama. Lily sat frozen until Joker went to her, pulling her roughly to her feet and shoving her toward the other women. Sex Piston grabbed Lily's arm before she could fall.

"Are you all right?" Sex Piston asked her.

Lily nodded her head, walking silently with the other women. When they were at the back of the salon in the small break room, Sex Piston knew it wasn't looking good for them. Both men's hatred was obvious as they stared at their exes with self-satisfied smirks. Neither one of the bastards could hold a job down, but they were proud as shit that they could hold them prisoners with guns. Both were too chicken shit to try to take them on without the lethal weapons.

"I'll watch them while you go get the money out of the register," Joker told Dale who then left the room.

"Joker, don't do this," Crazy Bitch said, trying to reach the man she had lived with for over a year. Sex Piston could have told her it was a lost cause, and his harsh words to her friend proved her correct.

"Do what, Crazy Bitch? You couldn't dump me fast enough when Stud and his men took over our club. You didn't care that you dumped me in front of my brothers. Why should I give a crap about you and your friends?"

Her friend tried to pacify the vindictive man. "I was going to call you to try to work things out."

"I don't want your crazy ass back. Hell, the only reason I put up with you was to keep a roof over my head. It would have been easier to work a ten-hour shift than to fuck around with you. Thanks to Sex Piston's money I won't have to do either for a while." The dumbass was actually bragging about being a lazy ass. Sex Piston wished she had the bat they kept in the backseat of their car. The bastard would be more than injured. The fucker would be dead.

"I don't keep much money in the register, just enough to make change. I wasn't leaving cash in my drawer for some lazy fuck to come in and rob me," Sex Piston told Joker, seeing her remark angered him. She was trying to draw his attention as Killyama tried to edge closer to him.

"She's telling the truth. She only has twenty dollars in the register," Dale said as he walked back into the room. He angrily walked up to T.A. "I thought you told me she had all kinds of money sitting around."

T.A. stared back defiantly. "Ever hear of bank deposits?"

Dale lifted his hand with the gun in it and smacked her

across her face. T.A. fell back against Lily who did her best to keep them from both falling. She was unsuccessful and they both fell to the floor hard.

"Get up!" Dale screamed, pointing the gun at T.A. "I didn't set half the town on fire for twenty dollars!"

"You started the fire?" Crazy Bitch asked.

"It's kept the cops busy, hasn't it?" Bending down, he grabbed a handful of T.A.'s hair and pulled the struggling woman to her feet. Lily rose slowly to her own feet, the cape around her tearing slightly as she stepped on it to regain her footing. She put out a trembling hand to smooth her hair away from her terrified face. Sex Piston noticed a lump on the side of her forehead from where she had hit her head when she had fallen.

"What are we going to do now?" Dale asked, moving backward to Joker as he carefully kept the women in his view.

"She's going to take you to the bank and withdraw some cash. If she tries anything, kill her." Pointing the gun at Sex Piston, he made his threat clear. "I'll kill one of these sluts every thirty minutes until you're back."

Sex Piston's blood ran cold at Joker's threat.

"Let's go." Dale motioned Sex Piston out the door.

Her thoughts raced as she tried to figure out a plan to free her friends. In her car they kept the bat, but the chances of her actually grabbing it or the weapons Killyama had in the trunk weren't very high when he had a gun pointed at her.

"Move your ass. And, Sex Piston, you try any shit with me and I'll make sure that I kill you then kill every one of those bitches waiting for you to come back," Dale ordered harshly.

Sex Piston gave him a cold glare as she slowly started to walk out of the room. "You always were a dick, Dale. You think I'm stupid enough that I haven't already figured out that you're planning on killing us anyway?"

The expression on his face confirmed her worst fears.

Chapter Fourteen

"I'll get you money," she gave in, figuring that she stood a better chance getting Dale alone than cramped into the small back room with two guns pointed at them.

It was better if they separated. Maybe one of them would be able to manage to escape. She caught Killyama and T.A.'s eyes, passing the silent message.

Sex Piston spun on her heels and walked to the front of the store, leading Dale through the empty shop. Unlocking the front door, she searched the parking lot with a quick glance.

"Lock the door back up," Dale ordered. Sex Piston took her shop keys out of her pocket.

"Move," she demanded him to get out of her way before turning back toward the door. After she locked the door, he jerked her away and pushed her toward her car parked on the side of the building. The parking lot was pitch black as she carefully walked so that she wouldn't trip in her high-heeled boots.

She opened her car door, forcing Dale to take a step back.

Hearing a shuffle, she looked over her shoulder to find

Stud's arm around Dale's neck from behind, holding him still while Shade took the gun out of his hand. Shade pointed the gun at Dale while Stud pressed against Dale's throat until he passed out. Stud let him fall to the ground.

Bear moved out of the shadows, picking up Dale as the other brothers from the club came out of the darkness.

"Put him somewhere and leave two men watching over him," Stud told Bear.

Sex Piston watched as they carried Dale off before turning back to Stud and Shade.

"You okay?" Stud asked.

She nodded, barely able to keep herself from throwing herself into his arms. She had learned to be tough long ago. Right now, she needed to keep her mind on her friends who were still in danger.

"Joker has the others in the back of the shop, Stud. He has a gun pointed on them," Sex Piston told them.

"We know." Stud grimly moved toward her to take her in his arms, holding her close. Sex Piston allowed herself a moment to relax against him.

"How?"

"Lily. We've been listening in on her cell phone," Shade answered.

Sex Piston thought of the cape around her, which would have hidden all her movements.

"Thank God." If she had removed the cape, then Joker and Dale would have taken the cell phone away. No one had thought of Lily having a cell phone in her pocket concealed by the large cape.

"Stay here." Stud released her after giving her a tight squeeze.

"I'm going with you. I can go in the door first and distract him," Sex Piston argued.

"You're staying here," he demanded, turning away, but she reached out and grabbed his arm, forcing him to listen to her.

"You've never been inside my shop. He has a gun on

my friends. You go through that door first, then Joker might shoot. Please, Stud." It took everything she had to plead with him. Any other time, she would just do what she wanted, but she wanted Stud to trust her enough to know what she was doing.

"Let her go. If he starts shooting in a small room, any of those women could be hit by a bullet. If she could get his back to the door, then we can take him," Shade said grimly.

Stud hesitated before nodding his head.

Sex Piston went to the door alone and unlocked it. Holding it open, the men moved silently into the shop. They moved behind the counter, trying to keep their reflections from the mirrors. At Shades nod, she walked toward the back of the shop, trying to beat down the panic flooding through her veins. She was aware Stud and Shade were maneuvering themselves closer to her.

Stud had a gun in his hand while Shade's remained empty, but the deadly look in his eyes made him every bit as frightening as Stud who carried the weapon with expert ease. Sex Piston released a long breath, letting the tension flow from her body. She had to be strong for her friends and for Lily. She had two deadly men at her back and numerous brothers converging on her shop.

She wasn't that same girl who had faced numerous challenges on her own; she hadn't been for a long time, but had never let herself truly realize it before. Strength and resolve shone on her face when she stepped into the doorway to face Joker.

He jerked the pistol toward her. Her eyes went to the others in the room. Joker had been amusing himself since she had left. She had been right; he had no intention of leaving any one of them alive. Crazy Bitch was on her knees on the floor; her lip bloodied and a bruise forming on her cheek. Killyama was holding Lily protectively; the cape she had been wearing was now gone and her hand cradled in the other one was a mangled mess.

T.A. and Fat Louise had separated and were standing on opposite sides of the room. Sex Piston knew they were waiting for the opportunity to attack Joker. None of her crew showed fear—they never had.

"Looks like you've been busy, Joker."

"Where's Dale?" he asked, his eyes going to the doorway behind her.

"He said to tell you to go fuck yourself, and took off," Sex Piston taunted the man.

"You're lying!"

"No, I'm not. When we got outside, he took off." Sex Piston shrugged, looking at T.A. "I always told you he was a pussy."

Sex Piston could see that Joker was torn in whether to believe her or not. Evidently, his doubt won out because he moved toward her. Sex Piston tried to move to the side so that she could get his back to the door, but Joker was too lost in his anger. Reacting violently to Dale's supposed departure, he grabbed Sex Piston, but before he could hit her, which was his intention, Killyama was on him. She had picked up one of the break chairs and crashed it down on the back of his head.

Stud and Shade were already running into the room, but Sex Piston couldn't get out of their way fast enough in the small room to keep Joker from blindly reacting. He fired his gun into the crowded room. It was the first time Sex Piston actually heard her crew scream in terror.

Shade managed to grab the gun away from Joker. Turning the gun to point directly at him, he fired a bullet into the side of Joker's abdomen.

"That will keep you busy." Shade's voice was as cold as his ice blue eyes.

Sex Piston looked around, praying silently. Her eyes went to Crazy Bitch who was getting to her feet. Lily shakily scooted closer to Fat Louise as T.A. rushed over to them. Fat Louise was lying on the floor, blood pouring from her leg. T.A. grabbed some towels from the shelf to try to stop the bleeding, and Lily sank down next to her, taking her hand with her good one. Her other hand fell uselessly to her lap.

Bear and Pike came in the door. "The state police are outside and an ambulance is on the way," Bear informed them.

Sex Piston went to her friend, going down on her knees beside her. Fat Louise's eyes rose to hers. Sex Piston's eyes watered, but she fought back tears.

"You're going to be okay," Sex Piston told her.

Fat Louise nodded, trusting her friend's judgment without question. She always had.

The women finally moved away as the ambulance technicians came through the door. It was too cramped in the small room, so everyone was forced to move outside to the shop as they worked on Fat Louise and checked on Lily who was turning pale. The red rubber band on her wrist, that was definitely broken, was a reminder that she might not be handling the situation as well as she seemed. The ambulance had removed Joker from the room to deal with his gunshot wound.

Two State Troopers came into the shop once the technicians cleared out. One approached Sex Pistol, asking questions, while the other went to Shade. She answered all of his questions as quickly as she could, wanting to be near her friend. Finally satisfied, the officer moved on to asking T.A. the same questions they had just asked her.

Killyama moved toward her when she saw the trooper turn to T.A., but Shade stopped her with a hand on her shoulder, ignoring the officer questioning him.

"I saw you putting yourself in front of Lily." His hard face stared at her friend. "Then you tried to take that bastard out before we could touch him. You still want that ride with Rider, it's yours."

Killyama's face broke into a vindictive smile. "I'll take you up on that, Shade."

Shaking his head, he turned back to the man

questioning him. The trooper had just finished questioning Shade when a stretcher with Lily on it was rolled out. He quickly followed them out the door, his facial expression daring anyone to try to stop him.

"I might have been wrong about that man," Killyama said.

"I doubt it," Sex Piston said. She had felt the tension in Shade when Lily's stretcher had rolled past. The man's muscles had bulged as his hands had clenched at his sides. The man was a ticking time bomb, and Sex Piston was grateful that The Last Riders were the ones that had to deal with that loose cannon.

Stud's arm circled her waist from behind. "You ready? The technician said you can ride with Fat Louise."

"Thanks, Stud." She turned her head, kissing him on his jaw before moving away to the ambulance that Fat Louise was being rolled into. She was confident her friends would lock up the shop after the police cleared out.

Climbing into the ambulance, she took a seat on the bench next to Fat Louise's stretcher. Her head turned and she saw the relief in the pretty gold eyes before they closed against her pale cheeks. Fat Louise was their weakest link, but sometimes their strongest. She was a total screw up at times and yet, whenever anyone needed something done that no one wanted to do, Fat Louise always came through.

She was the one that knew the most about what Sex Piston had gone through when she had been bullied in middle school because she had experienced it herself before Crazy Bitch and Killyama had taken her under their wing.

The ride to the hospital was short and she became increasingly concerned when she heard over the intercom—in which the drivers of the two ambulances talked to each other—that Lily had lost consciousness. The lights on the ambulance behind them began blaring and then gaining speed while theirs slowed so the other could overtake them, speeding away.

Fat Louise and her stared at each other, worried about Beth's sister. She was a sweet woman who Beth obviously worshiped and had raised since their parents' death.

The ambulance pulled into the hospital and they rolled Fat Louise's stretcher from the vehicle, telling Sex Piston to do the required paperwork then wait in the waiting room. Sex Piston wanted to argue, but knew it would do no good.

Giving her friend a quick word of encouragement, she went to find the check-in counter, which was easy to do since the commotion hit her when she walked in through the sliding doors.

Utter chaos was taking place in the form of Shade, who was trying to get inside where the patients were being treated. Two security officers were holding him back, threatening to place him under arrest.

"Shit." Sex Piston rushed forward as he slammed the men together, knocking them on their asses.

"Shade," Sex Piston tried to intervene then thought better of it when she saw his face.

The sliding doors opened behind her and Stud, Viper and Razer entered to find her trying to deal with a crazed Shade.

Razer and Viper took on Shade while Stud helped the security guards to their feet. Taking them to the side, she could see him talking quietly to them. Razer and Viper were both attempting unsuccessfully to stop Shade from going into the room where Lily was being treated. Shade shook off Viper then rounded on Razer, throwing him up against the wall, his forearm pressed against Razer's throat.

"I'm fucking done. You hear me, Razer?" Razer managed to nod his head against the pressure Shade was exerting against his throat. "That woman in there could die. I haven't even been able to touch her yet, feel her against me, or even fucking kiss her because I've let what little conscience I have left, and my friendship with you, stop me. No more. You deal with Beth however you want, but I'm done with everyone telling me to stay away from her. Do you fucking understand me?" Again Razer nodded.

Shade stepped back, moving away from both Viper and Razer who stood watching, like her, as Shade fought for control. Running a shaking hand over his short-cropped hair, he finally managed to regain control over himself before turning back to his brothers, catching sight of Sex Piston.

The sudden blaring over the intercom calling a code had his eyes going wild again. Sex Piston took a step forward before he could lose it again, grabbing him by the front of his shirt.

"You need to get your shit under control," she said between gritted teeth. "Beth will come in that door any minute." Her eyes swept to the side, seeing Razer's confirming nod. "Lily will not be happy to have her sister upset any more than she already is. So calm your ass down." Sex Piston saw that her words were getting through to the hardass biker.

"I see what you see in her. She comes across as this frail as shit wimp until you look in her eyes. She's strong, Shade. Strong enough to survive whatever hell that's been given to her. She *will* pull out of this. She will never forgive you if you hurt anyone she cares about."

"You can't be sure she'll be all right!" he said harshly as several hospital staff ran into the room Lily was in.

"Yes, I do." She lifted her shirt from the hem, baring her tattoos to his gaze. Her finger touched the two butterfly tats, drawing his gaze to her side. "I was stabbed twice when I was in the seventh grade, Shade. I coded twice. I'm standing before you now, telling you that beautiful girl is not going to die." No doubt was in her gaze.

Shade calmed as he leaned back against the wall for support. Sex Piston gave him a sharp nod. "You cool now?"

"Yeah, I'm cool," Shade said, his eyes on the doorway, but he made no more attempts to go inside.

Sex Piston went to Stud, feeling his strength when his arm slid around her shoulders. He pulled her to his side, and Sex Piston shuddered against him, having relived the traumatic experience of her youth. He buried his face in the curve of her neck, letting his warmth sink in to her flesh, warming her.

The sliding doors opened again, and Killyama, Crazy Bitch and T.A. came in, worried about Fat Louise and Lily.

"We don't know anything yet," Sex Piston explained before they could ask. "Did you call her mother?"

"Yes, she said to call her when we know something." Disgust for Fat Louise's mother was not new to them. They all looked at the doorway as Beth and The Last Rider's women and brothers came into the waiting room. Diamond and Knox, wearing a deputy outfit, surprised her.

Beth went directly to Razer. "How is she?"

Sex Piston couldn't hear his answer, but she saw the effect of it on her friend. Beth crumpled, almost falling to the floor before she was caught against her husband and held tight against his body. Sex Piston heard the cries of the women and wanted to join them, only her iron control held it back. She couldn't bear the thought of crying in front of other women.

It was two hours later before a tired doctor came out to talk to them.

"Lily is going to be okay, but it was close. She had an epidural hematoma. We relieved the pressure and she's stable for now. If she had been a minute further away from the hospital, she wouldn't have made it." The doctor ran a hand over his face, exhaustion apparent. "Her hand is broken in two places. We've stabilized the hand for now and we'll put a cast on it in the morning." His words let everyone know she was still in critical condition.

"How about Fa—" Crazy Bitch cleared her throat. "What about Louise?"

"She's in surgery to remove the bullet, but it did little damage." The doctor turned to go back into the room. "Only two family members can go into see Miss Cornett before she's moved to the ICU. Make it quick. She isn't conscious, but I'm sure you're anxious to see her." The Doctor went back into the emergency room.

Beth went to the door the doctor had already gone through, opening it before turning back. Tears rolling down her cheeks, she held out her hand toward Shade. Sex Piston sucked in a startled breath as he took a step forward, taking her hand. They went into the E.R. together, the door closing behind them, leaving a stunned silence behind them.

"I guess she figured it out," Winter said, smiling at her husband.

"I don't know whether to be relieved or worried," Viper replied, smiling back at Winter before looking at Razer who gave a shrug in answer.

"They're both going to be okay," Sex Piston said in relief. She glanced around the room. "How did you get rid of the security guards?"

It didn't take Stud a second to answer—without any conscience—that he had bribed them with cash and women. "Five hundred apiece, and I told them they could come by the clubhouse this weekend."

"What's going on at the clubhouse this weekend?" she asked, trying to remember if anything special was going on.

"Not a damn thing," he replied.

Chapter Fifteen

"They're going to let you out of here tomorrow," Crazy Bitch said, swiping a chicken leg from the boxed dinner sitting in front of Fat Louise.

"I talked to the doctor; he said I might need to stay a day or two longer," Fat Louise replied, digging into her Popeye's chicken dinner for another piece of chicken.

"Why's that?" Sex Piston asked from the bottom of her bed. She was sitting casually on the bed, watching her friend eat the dinner that Killyama had sneaked in for the third day in a row.

"I told him that I was feeling a sharp pain and he wants to make sure there are no compilations so he's going to keep me hospitalized." Fat Louise wiped her greasy fingers on her napkin.

Sex Piston's lips twitched, her friend was milking her stay for everything she was worth. T.A. had even been sneaking in her favorite birthday cake milkshakes. She also had Killyama bring her favorite meal of year, and Crazy Bitch keeping her constant company. The girl had no intention of getting better soon. If the hot as hell doctor kept visiting her between rounds, Sex Piston was afraid the woman would fake a coma to stay.

"Did you stop in to see Lily before she left?" Fat Louise asked.

"Yes. Unlike you, she was anxious to go home," Sex Piston said softly. Because Beth and Evie were both skilled nurses, the doctor had been convinced to release her that afternoon, but she would be under the care of a physician for several weeks.

Fat Louise lowered her eyes. "I'd want to leave, too, if I had Beth, Razer and Shade waiting on me to leave."

"*We're* waiting for you to leave," Sex Piston consoled, her hand going to her friend's foot, giving it a playful squeeze.

Another shrug was her response. "My mom's not."

"I already talked to your mom. I packed your shit up and moved it to my house. You're going to live with me for a while, if you don't mind. Now that Joker doesn't live with me anymore, I get lonely. You can keep me company," Crazy Bitch said, sitting down on the bed beside her.

"For real?" Fat Louise perked up immediately.

"For real," Crazy Bitch confirmed with a smile. "Besides, now that you have a job you can pay half the rent which is more than Joker ever did."

"I can do that," Fat Louise said in agreement.

Sex Piston stood up and smoothed down the bed sheets. "I've got to go. I'm meeting Stud for dinner at his house."

"Say hi to the girls for me." Fat Louise waved her off with a drumstick.

Saying goodbye to her friends, Sex Piston walked out of the small hospital. She still felt moments of relief that Lily and Fat Louise had survived when the outcome could have been one or all of them dead. If she had taken the cape off Lily… If Lily hadn't had her cell phone in her pocket… She was just thankful this time the circumstances were in their favor. Unfortunately, that also meant several more months of Popeye's.

Sex Piston drove to Stud's house. Her nerves—she would have sworn she didn't have—began kicking in, making her nervous about the coming meeting. She was meeting his aunt tonight, who was very important to him.

Sex Piston pulled into Stud's driveway, sucking in a deep breath before she walked to his door.

Before she could knock, the door was opened and Meri stood there, staring up at her with a big smile.

"Hi, Sex Piston."

"Meri!" an admonishing voice came from the kitchen.

Sex Piston winked at the girl, coming in and shutting the door behind her. She saw Stud's aunt enter the living room, coming to a stop when she saw Sex Piston.

Her shocked eyes went over her tight leather leggings and oversized sweater that dipped low enough to show the globes of her breasts. Her black leather, studded jacket, and skull rings only added to the image of the classic biker bitch. Stud's aunt didn't try to hide her disappointment, her lips tightening in disappointment.

"You must be Stud's friend, Sex Piston." Sex Piston could tell the woman was having difficulty getting her name to come out of her mouth.

"You must be Stud's Aunt Katy," Sex Piston returned the introduction, holding out her hand with the bright red fingernails and skull ring on.

She could tell the woman was afraid she would catch something if she touched her. Briefly she shook her hand then took a step away, wiping her hand on the side of her apron.

"Stud called and said he was running late. Have a seat while I finish dinner."

"Can I help? I'm—"

"No. Um, I have it under control. You keep Meri and Keri company. Meri, go get your sister," she said hurriedly. "I better get back in the kitchen. I don't want anything to burn." The woman skedaddled as if she had a porcupine up her ass. Sex Piston sat down on the couch while Meri went in search of her sister.

Movement from Star's playpen drew Sex Piston's gaze as Star toddled to the end of the playpen and stood, grasping it while she stared at her as she sucked her thumb.

"Sexy!" she squealed. A revealing smile broke free as Sex Piston stood up to pick up the toddler. Her baby powder smell enveloped her as she held her. Those chubby little arms circled her neck, grasping handfuls of her hair and tugging.

"Whatcha doing, Star? You being a good girl for your aunt?" Sex Piston cooed, going back to take her seat on the couch.

Sitting the girl on her lap, the little girl's hands went over her leather jacket, playing with the zipper. Sex Piston baby talked with her for several minutes until she saw a movement from the kitchen doorway.

"Dinner's ready," Katy said with a smile. "Why don't you put Star in her highchair and I'll give you her bowl to feed her?"

"Sounds good," Sex Piston said, rising with the little girl in her arms.

Going into the kitchen, she put Star in the highchair that was already placed at the table. Sex Piston sat down in the chair next to it, taking the bowl of vegetable soup that Stud's aunt handed her.

"I already let it cool," she said in amusement when she saw Sex Piston testing the warmth of the soup.

"Okay."

Sex Piston was feeding Star her third spoonful when Stud walked in with Meri and Keri by his side.

"I see you've met," Stud said while he and his daughters took their place at the table.

"Yes," Katy answered, placing bowls of soup in front of each of them. A big plate of cornbread followed with a big plate of club sandwiches.

Katy took her own seat, while Sex Piston continued to

feed Star as she ate her own food. When the little girl became restless, Sex Piston handed her a cracker to play with.

"Do you have any children, Sex Piston?" Stud's aunt asked casually.

"No," She answered.

"You're very good with children," Katy remarked.

"I babysat while I was in high school. I have a lot of cousins who are younger than me." She shrugged.

"How was school today, girls?" Stud asked, taking another piece of cornbread.

"Good," Meri said, looking at Sex Piston from underneath her lashes.

"It's nice of your friend to pick the girls up from school. Now that I'm here with Stud, they can ride the bus. I could pick them up, but I don't like driving with Star in the car. I get distracted when she gets fussy."

"It's no problem. Killyama doesn't mind," Sex Piston said, getting up from the table to get paper towels to clean the mess that Star was making with her cracker.

"Kill-ya-ma?" Katy asked with a concerned look.

"She's great, Aunt Katy. She's kind of scary, but she's really nice. She lets us stop on the way home to get an ice cream cone," Keri said.

"You're not supposed to tell. She said Aunt Katy might not like us eating ice cream every day," Meri scolded her sister, concerned she would lose the special treat.

Katy smothered her laughter, her concerned look gone. "Yes, well, it's not very good for dinner, but I don't suppose it will hurt if you play for thirty minutes when you both get home instead of watching television."

Meri and Keri looked glumly at each other while their aunt began to gather the dirty bowls, placing them in the sink.

"I'll do the dishes," Sex Piston volunteered.

"That will be a help. I'll give Star her bath." Katy carried a fussy Star out of the room.

"We have homework," Meri said as her and her sister left the kitchen.

"You came earlier than we planned," Stud stated as he began doing the dishes.

"I finished early at work."

"You go by the hospital first?"

"Yeah." Sex Piston wiped down the table then tossed the cloth onto the counter.

"How was Lily?"

"One fucked up mess." She could still picture Lily's frozen expression in her mind as she left the hospital surrounded by The Last Riders. Her hand was in a cast that seemed to weigh a ton on the delicate woman.

"Fat Louise?"

"Working it for everything she can. She's so spoilt she doesn't want to leave the hospital." Sex Piston's expression lightened.

Stud laughed. "You sleeping in her room all night is a little excessive."

"Fat Louise gets lonely."

"When would she get lonely with one of you always around." He placed the dishtowel down on the counter. Sex Piston wiped down the counters while Stud moved the highchair back into the corner.

"You need to find a bigger place now that your aunt has moved in." Sex Piston watched his reaction from the corner of her eye.

"No need to. My place in West Virginia is big enough for us all," Stud said, putting the leftover soup into the fridge.

Sex Piston paused after putting the cloth on the counter.

"What are we doing here, Stud?"

Stud looked at her quizzically. "We're cleaning the kitchen?"

"No." Beginning to get angry, she pointed first at him then at herself. "Me and you. Where are we going? You said we're not fuck buddies, yet you intend to go back to West Virginia?"

Stud stared back at her intently until Sex Piston had enough when he remained silent.

"Fuck this." Spinning around, she was about to leave, but his voice stopped her.

"Sex Piston, I own my home in West Virginia. It's big enough for all of us. My family and the Blue Horsemen are there, not here."

"I have my family here, my sisters are here, my business is here. Knox gave up being the biggest horndog in The Last Riders for Diamond and he bought her a fucking island."

"Why did he buy her an island?" Stud asked in amazement.

"Because she's afraid of zombies."

"Zombies?"

"Zombies can't swim, so he bought her an island," Sex Piston explained her sister's logic.

"They can't?" Stud looked like he was actually debating the issue in his mind.

"How the hell would I know!" Sex Piston yelled. "The point is, he made a change in his life for Diamond." Her arms crossed over her chest as she glared at him.

"I'm not buying you a fucking island!" Stud looked at her as if she had lost her mind. The jerk didn't have a romantic bone in his body.

"I don't want you to buy me a fucking island!" Sex Piston yelled, angry at herself for trying to find out how Stud felt about her while she couldn't make up her own mind if she was going to keep him or not.

Katy came rushing into the kitchen. "What in the world is going on in here? The children can hear your language in the other room."

"I need to go home. See you later, Stud." Sex Piston rushed from the kitchen, going to the front door. She managed to get into her car before Stud got to the door with Katy by his side. She bit down hard on her lip as she reversed out of the driveway.

Driving in the direction of the hospital, she steeled herself against the turmoil of emotions trying to break free inside of her, determined to hold the hurt and anger at bay. She had learned long ago how to smother any emotions that threatened to break through the guards she had built around her heart.

She had wanted to find out how Stud felt about her and where they were heading before loosening her grip on her heart. It was a good thing she found out now before she had fallen for the asshole. She unconsciously wiped a tear away that had slid down her cheek. The bastard could find another fuck buddy to keep him busy until he went home to West Virginia for all she cared. She told herself this all the way back to the hospital, entering Fat Louise's room to find her entire crew still there.

They didn't ask why she was back so soon. Instead, they handed her one of the beers Crazy Bitch had snuck in and then they spent the night watching a zombie movie on Fat Louise's laptop. When it was over, she was still mad as hell at Stud, but she began to wonder if Diamond had been smoking any of the green Shade was always buying for The Last Riders.

Chapter Sixteen

Stud leaned against the bar at the Destructors' clubhouse, barely managing to restrain himself from walking across the room and dragging Sex Piston into his room. She had been ignoring him for the past few days, since their argument at his house.

He had no intention of leaving the woman he cared about behind while he went back to West Virginia. He had been attempting to see if she had begun to have any deep feelings for him. Instead, it had backfired and she had stormed out on him while he had tried to calm down his aunt.

Sex Piston concerned his aunt because she was familiar with both his ex-wife and Star's mother. Sex Piston seemed worse with her attitude than both of them together. Stud knew she had no reason for concern; Sex Piston was the exact opposite of the other women. They only were concerned about themselves while Sex Piston gave everything to everyone else; sacrificing her own wants and needs.

"You going to put up with that shit?" Bear remarked by his side as Jace walked up to Sex Piston's table to ask her to dance. He watched as she got to her feet, leaving her friends at their table as she seductively glided to the dance floor on those high heels that she managed to walk on, defying gravity.

She was dressed to draw every man's eyes to her body in a black dress. It had black netting around her shoulders, a patch of black leather just wide enough to cover her breasts, and another patch of black netting circled her flat stomach before a second circle of black leather covered her from her hips downward to the top of her thighs.

Stud swallowed a long drink of beer, his cock hardening behind his jeans. Moving uncomfortably, he sat the beer slowly back down on the bar when he really wanted to smash it against Jace's smug face as his hand went to Sex Piston's hip, pulling her close.

The security guards' radios went off simultaneously. Stud looked across the bar at them as their radios blared a warning signal. Both men stood up, leaving in a hurry. Stud wondered what could have lit a fire under their asses to have both of them running out of the clubhouse. The TV above the bar gave a warning as the thought crossed his mind.

Stud read the warning; an Amber Alert had been issued. A toddler had been kidnapped from a local home. Stud read the description. The child was thought to be in the custody of her mother.

His cell phone distracted him from reading the rest of the alert message. Answering it, he heard his aunt screaming hysterically into the phone.

"Slow down; I can't understand you…" Stud listened to Aunt Katy describe Star's mother coming by for a visit. Katy could tell she was high as a kite and refused to let her hold Star. Candi had attacked her, knocking her down to the floor. She had grabbed Star and took off. Stud heard Meri and Keri screaming and crying in the background.

"I'll find her, Katy. Calm the girls down. I swear I'll find her." Stud hung up from his aunt, his hand clutching the bar in both terror for his daughter and fury at Candi for endangering Star by driving with the baby when she was stoned.

Stud turned to Bear, realizing the Club had gone quiet, listening to his conversation. All knew that something terrible had happened, if not the exact details.

"What's up?" Bear asked as his brothers listened unashamedly.

"Candi took Star." Stud gathered his thoughts so that he could make a plan. He opened his mouth, directing his brothers, taking command while holding his fear for his daughter at bay.

"Pike, take Jace. Go to Candi's place and call me as soon as you get there. Rock and Blade, separate and hit every dealer; see if they know of any place she would hide. Dozer, go to the bridge crossing over to Treepoint, keep an eye out for her car. The rest of us are going to split up and hit the other way out of town."

The brothers filed out of the clubhouse. Stud went out the door, hearing Sex Piston call his name, but he kept going. He had to find his daughter then he would deal with Sex Piston.

He came to a stop when he got outside. The brothers were also stopped in their tracks, looking at the woman walking unsteadily across the parking lot.

"I was coming to see you, Stud!" Candi called out to him, holding a crying Star.

"Give her to me, Candi. You're scaring her." Stud took a step toward her, but stopped suddenly. Candi had started backing up when she saw the large number of members coming out of the club. She was almost up to the edge of the parking lot which had a drop off of about six feet. At the bottom was a small creek that ran behind the club.

Stud had talked to Skulls about getting it fenced off; concerned one of the brothers would drunkenly fall off. Skulls had shrugged and said it wouldn't be the first time. It was then that Stud knew the extent of what Sex Piston had grown up in. Skulls was a good man and biker, but he was careless where safety was concerned.

"Listen to me, Stud." She took another step back.

Stud stood still. "I'm listening."

"I want Star back. I *need* her," Candi whined.

"We'll talk about it. We can work something out." Stud would promise her anything to get Star to safety.

Candi started rubbing Star's hair, trying to soothe the terrified girl. Stud was afraid to take another step forward for fear of her falling over the embankment.

"Candi, how you doing? It's been awhile since I've seen you around." Stud watched as Sex Piston came up beside him.

"Sex Piston, is that you?"

"Yeah, it's me, Candi. I've been wondering where you've been." Sex Piston moved a few inches away from Stud.

"I heard about you and Stud. He won't let me have my kid. He's got to listen to me," Candi said, almost losing her balance when she switched Star to her other hip.

"I think he's listening to you now, Candi." Sex Piston took another step away from Stud, moving more toward the left side of the parking lot away from the clubhouse. Candi's eyes followed her, but she kept switching back and forth between her and Stud, keeping both of them within her sights.

"You look worn out; want to have a seat in my car and rest for a minute until you're feeling better? I could hold Star for you."

"You're trying to take my Star now that you got Stud. My baby doesn't need you playing mommy. She already has one." She poked herself with her finger. "I'm her mother. She doesn't need another one of his sluts pretending to be."

"I know that you're her mother, Candi. Every time I look at her I see your pretty eyes. She looks a lot like you."

Stud watch as Killyama moved stealthy to the side,

sneaking up from the back of the building, moving through the shadows so that Candi couldn't see her.

Star started crying harder. It broke something in Sex Piston that she didn't think could be broken anymore.

Stud could only watch in admiration as Sex Piston tried to lure Candi away from the embankment.

"Sexy. I want Sexy," his daughter cried, holding out her arms to Sex Piston.

"Shut up, Star," Candi screamed at her daughter.

"Candi," calmly Sex Piston held out her arms, terror on her face, "please, please let that baby go. You're scaring her."

Stud was standing there, watching the woman he loved drop all her guards and pride to get Star safe.

"What the hell do you care?"

"I love her, and I'm begging you to hand me Star because you're her mother and when you're not drugged out of your fucking mind, you're going to be sick at how much danger you've put her in tonight."

Candi stopped weaving for a split second, her gaze never leaving Sex Piston's tear-streaked face.

"Please, Candi, I'm begging you. Give her to me." Sex Piston took a step forward and Candi started to take another step back, but came up against Killyama who braced her weight steady before putting her hands in her hair, tugging her head backward at an awkward angle.

"You're going to stand still and gently give that baby to Sex Piston right now because if you don't, you stupid bitch, I'm going to break your fucking neck and take her out of your cold, dead hands." Killyama's cold and concise voice saved Candi's life, giving her a moment's clarity long enough not to resist Sex Piston when she took Star away from her.

As soon as Sex Piston got the baby away, Killyama threw Candi roughly to the ground, grinding her face into the gravel of the parking lot several times before Pike and Blade could pull the vicious woman away.

Stud went to Sex Piston, wanting desperately to hold his daughter, but he saw he would have to wait in line. He had wondered and always somehow knew Sex Piston's capacity for love; now it was on display before him.

She was on her knees in the graveled parking lot, holding Star to her chest, crying into her neck as if her world was shattered. Crazy Bitch, Fat Louise, T.A. and then Killyama surrounded her, trying to give her privacy until she could regain control. When Stud saw her friends look of concern, he knew that Sex Piston had never even shown this side to them.

"Sex Piston." Stud went to her, going down on his haunches beside her, his hand rubbing Star's curls. "She's safe. You're holding her, and she's safe." A shuddering breath had her nodding her head as she turned sideways, handing him Star.

Stud got to his feet before reaching down and helping Sex Piston get to hers. Several police cars drove onto the parking lot, screeching to a stop. Their lights bright in the dark night.

Sex Piston's hands smoothed away her tears as she went to her car. Her crew following closely behind her. Stud wanted to stop her from leaving, but knew he had to talk to the police and straighten out the mess Candi had made.

Sighing in regret, he turned back to the officers as they approached. Star's arms twined around his neck. Relief at her being safe brought tears to his own eyes.

Right now, all his women needed him, but he had to take care of the bullshit that Candi had created first before he could restore order and reassure them that everything was okay, including the woman who had driven away without a backward glance.

She didn't know that it was the last time she would be walking away from him.

Chapter Seventeen

Sex Piston stood beside her sister in the tiny clerk's office. She had answered her phone that morning to her sister's voice filled with laughter as she told her to get her ass to the courthouse and bring Ma and Pops if they wanted to see her get married.

She had jumped out of bed and called her crew, setting up a small reception for them afterward at the clubhouse before getting herself dressed. She had managed to get Ma and Pops organized enough to get them all there with five minutes to spare.

The small room was already filled to capacity with Viper, Diamond, Razer, Beth, Lily, Shade, Rider and Train. Diamond gave her a happy smile as the judge began. It was short and sweet with the happy couple kissing each other before Diamond turned to their parents, giving each of them a hug.

Sex Piston managed to maneuver herself through the crowd to give her sister a brief hug before telling her that she had set up the reception for her. Diamond gave her a grateful smile before telling everyone in the room.

The drive back to Jamestown thankfully gave her

friends time enough to gather the needed supplies for the unplanned celebration. When Sex Piston and her parents walked in the door, she was happy with the results that had been accomplished in such a short time.

Stud and all the Destructors that Diamond had grown up with had been told, plus the Blue Horseman had every intention of taking part if liquor was provided. Many had left work early for the chance to party.

Sex Piston hadn't seen Stud since Candi had pulled her stunt with Star. Skulls had told her that Stud had spent the last two days trying to get help for Candi while at the same time legally protecting Star's rights, making sure Candi would never get near Star again.

She found a table before all of them could be taken. Crazy Bitch and Killyama took a seat, having grabbed the beer.

"Think she's knocked up?" Crazy Bitch asked.

"No, Diamond would plan on getting pregnant three years in advance," Sex Piston answered her.

A chair was pulled out and Stud took a seat next to her. All the women stared at him as he placed a casual arm across the back of her chair. Diamond sat down on her other side.

"Next time, give us a little warning, Diamond," Sex Piston told her sister while ignoring Stud's possessive behavior.

"There's not going to be a next time," laughed Diamond, not getting upset at her sister's snarky remark. She reached into her pocket and pulled out a slip of paper, handing it to Sex Piston.

Curiously, she opened it to find it was a check. The amount had her eyes opening wide as she stared at Diamond in surprise.

"Who you wanting me to kill?" Sex Piston asked, not understanding why Diamond would give her so much money.

"No one. That's to pay you back. I tried to give it to

Mom and Dad." Her smile disappeared before she reached out and took Sex Piston's hand. "They told me you were the one to help pay for my college. All those babysitting jobs you took; you gave Ma the money for me. You even dropped out of high school senior year despite Ma and Pops begging you not to get a full time job.

"It took three times as long for you to get through beauty school because you were still giving Ma your money for me." Diamond's eyes shone with love for Sex Piston as she recounted Sex Piston's sacrifices for her.

"I didn't know, and all those times I was bitching at you for not educating yourself better, you just ignored me." Diamond bit her lip, gazing at her little sister.

"You were a better sister to me than I was to you. I was the older one and I should have watched out for you. I failed you, Sex Piston, and I'm deeply ashamed. I thought you were the one instigating the fights, stealing all the girls' boyfriends. Instead, it was the other way around and you were protecting me to keep me from getting hurt again.

"I owe you my law degree, and even the life I'll be leading with Knox. I would have never gotten to know him if I hadn't had to take his case. That money will never equal the life you have given me. Thank you."

Sex Piston couldn't say anything around the lump in her throat, finally just managing to give a smile.

"I'm so proud of you," Diamond told her.

"Enough to let me have a spot on your island if zombies attack?" Sex Piston joked.

"You know it," Diamond said seriously.

"You guys are creeping me the fuck out. I need another beer," Killyama said, getting to her feet.

Knox came to their table. "Let's dance."

"Okay." Diamond stood up. She leaned down, hugging her sister close before letting her go.

Knox gazed down at his new sister-in-law and pulled her to her feet before pulling her into a bear hug. "I'm a lucky man. I married a woman I love and now I have a sister. I've never had a family, Sex Piston, and I plan on enjoying having you and your parents as mine." His bald-headed badassness was ruined by the twinkle in his eyes. "Especially if you're the one who cooks when we have dinner at your parents' house."

"I think I can manage that."

Killyama, who had returned with her beer, turned on her heel again. "Pike, get your ass over here and dance with me. I can't handle all this mushy bullshit."

Sex Piston grinned at Killyama's abrasive behavior. Knox grinned, too, as he took Diamond's hand and led her to the dance floor. Sex Piston sat back down at the table where Stud's arm was still around the back of her chair.

Crazy Bitch stared at them a moment before yelling, "Blade!" Giving a wicked grin, she also took off to the dance floor. Blade joined her with a frightened look.

"Your men are pussies," she said, watching Pike dance as far away from Killyama as he could.

"Do you blame them?" Stud asked.

"No, both Crazy Bitch and Killyama could take them," Sex Piston bragged.

Bear sat down at the table, pulling T.A. down to sit on his lap. Fat Louise tried to cut in with Pike and Killyama, but two of the biker bitches were more than he could handle and he retreated back to the bar.

Later, Sex Piston and everyone else in the bar cheered when the happy couple left for their honeymoon. They were riding Knox's bike to Florida to see their new island.

Sex Piston seriously needed to find out who Shade was buying his reefer from.

Chapter Eighteen

"Let's get out of here." Stud took her hand, dragging her from the club without giving her a chance to tell her crew she was leaving.

Stud's bike was parked outside. Sex Piston climbed on behind him and then the bike roared out of the parking lot, making Sex Piston cling tighter to Stud, scooting closer to him on the seat so that her thighs could nestle next to his. The friction of his jeans against her bare thighs had Sex Piston's body reminding her that they hadn't fucked since before the argument the night she had met his aunt.

Star's kidnapping had kept him busy and she hadn't gone over to his house to see the girls. She had wanted to regroup, but this time it was harder to do. Star had made her realize that she couldn't keep Stud out of her heart because he was already there.

Sex Piston dragged herself from her thoughts, realizing that they were going out of Jamestown and heading toward Treepoint. Sex Piston enjoyed the ride, wishing she could enjoy the wind rushing by, but her pops had only instilled one rule when he had taught her to ride and that was to always ride with a helmet.

Expecting to go directly to Treepoint, Sex Piston was surprised when Stud turned at a side road that led up a winding path of one of the mountains. She had seen the turn off several times on the way to see Beth, but had never paid it much attention.

He followed the curvy road that gradually grew steeper and steeper. Sex Piston's hold tightened even further at the sheer drop off on the side of the road, but her confidence in Stud never faltered. Even when a deer ran across the road, he handled the bike with expert precision.

After fifteen minutes, he slowed down, taking an even smaller side road for about a half mile before pulling onto a long driveway that had a gated entrance. Stud pulled his bike up to a metal box that he inserted a key into. The heavy gate slid open and Stud's bike drove through the entrance.

The house she saw was everything you would expect from a home in the mountain. It was a two-story log home with a wraparound porch. The back of the house hung off the side of the mountain, and Sex Piston could only imagine that the views from the deck would be spectacular.

"Where are we?" Sex Piston asked as they climbed off the bike.

"My home."

"You live here?" Sex Piston couldn't understand how he could afford a home like this.

He was working at Powell's garage in town as a mechanic until he got the Destructors settled. She had assumed that was what he did in West Virginia. Sex Piston couldn't imagine him working a nine to five job, so that left only one option. She had found herself a dud. There was no way that he could afford a home like this on a mechanic's salary; he was involved in some illegal shit.

"Take me home."

They had been walking to his front door, but he came to a sudden stop at her angry command.

"Why don't you want to see my home?" She could tell

he wasn't going to take her back to Jamestown without her going inside first.

"Because I don't want to know how you paid for it. It would make me an accessory, and I don't plan on visiting you in jail!"

Stud laughed while continuing on to the house, keeping his hand on her arm while she kept trying to get away. When the door closed behind them, he let her go.

Sex Piston closed her open mouth with a snap. No wonder he had refused to get a bigger place when she had suggested it. He already owned a huge home.

Despite her hesitance, Sex Piston wandered through his house. The living room was large with a stone fireplace and wooden floors. The heavy furniture fit in with the rustic style of the log home. Sex Piston knew the furniture was expensive. She was planning on giving her mother a new living room set for Mother's Day. This was the furniture that when she told the salesmen her budget, he would walk on by to the room at the back of the store which held the cheaper sets.

The eat-in kitchen was just as big as the living room, with a table sitting by the double glass doors which had another beautiful view off the deck. She could imagine Stud and the girls eating breakfast there with the doors open.

She felt the lump in her throat get bigger as she walked throughout Stud's home with him following behind. She found Aunt Katy's room; it was next to the kitchen beside the laundry room.

She went up the steps to the second floor. The first bedroom had twin beds and pale pink walls. The lace curtains blew in the wind from the open window. Sex Piston went to the girls' dresser they shared, picking up the red ribbon that she had seen in Meri's hair then the purple one she had seen in Keri's. She looked at Stud standing in the doorway, watching. He moved back as she went through the door, closing it behind her.

The room she saw next to the girls' was Star's nursery. The pale yellow and green walls with cartoon characters playing were adorable. She walked to her crib and saw a tan rabbit lying there. She reached in, taking the rabbit and brushing it against her cheek, smelling Star's distinctive baby powder smell.

She left Star's room reluctantly, going to the room across the hall. She opened that door and saw a room with pale, tan walls and a large bed and dresser, but it was otherwise impersonal. She closed the door to Stud's guest room without bothering to go inside.

Sex Piston paused before opening the last door, knowing it was Stud's. Taking a deep breath, she opened the door. The room was the largest of them all, decorated with different shades of browns and green. It had a fireplace that was in the corner of the room, designed— Sex Piston was sure—so that you could lie on the bed and still have a view of the fireplace.

"You're home is beautiful, Stud." Sex Piston's husky voice was soft in the quietness of the house. She walked to the window, pulling back the cream-colored sheers, looking at the beauty of the surrounding mountains.

"Thank you."

Sex Piston laid her forehead against the window pane, closing her eyes. She felt Stud come up behind her, slipping his arms around her waist.

"I had a friend when I was younger. We were friends from the first day of school, Stud. Ma still has pictures of us in school, sitting together that first day of kindergarten. We were best friends all the way through elementary school. She had started school late because of her birthday and she hadn't passed kindergarten the first time, so she was older than me, but she didn't act it. I looked up to her because she already knew everything. I followed her around like a puppy for years."

Sex Piston hesitated then continued with her story. "The first day of sixth grade, she changed. She became friends with girls in the seventh and eighth grades. I was small for my age, but developed. The boys and girls noticed. My friend started hanging out with her new friends, but they wouldn't let me. They were mean, called me names and basically tortured me throughout middle school.

"I didn't tell anyone, Stud. Not Ma or Pops, or even Diamond. The girls really didn't like the boys paying attention to me. One day, I made the mistake of letting one of the boys walk me home from school. The next day at school, they were horrible to me, but I pretended to ignore them the way I always did.

"It was raining that day, so I rode the bus home. My friend motioned for me to sit with her at the back of the bus. She was smiling and waving at me, like when we were little. I went and sat down next to them. As soon as the bus started moving, they ganged up on me.

"The one that stabbed me twice had a crush on the boy who walked me home. She wanted to teach me a lesson. I learned my lesson that day, Stud, and I never forgot it. Allison didn't participate, but she watched. She didn't try to help me. She even stood in front of the back mirror so that the bus driver couldn't see that six girls were beating me to death."

Stud tightened his hold on her. "What happened?"

A smile touched her lips. "Killyama, Crazy Bitch, T.A. and even Fat Louise took them all on. They were hurt, too, but they managed to get the bus driver's attention, and get the girls away from me. Killyama held my jacket against my side until they could get an ambulance. Ma told me they stayed at the hospital until her and Pops could get there. We became friends that day and it's lasted all these years.

"I always imagined the man I fell in love with would live in Jamestown. We'd buy a home not far from Ma and Pops house, close enough for me to go by their house everyday and take care of things for them. I would always be able to go by the club for a beer with Killyama, Crazy

Bitch, Fat Louise and T.A. Go running around with them in our car, have kids together, get old together."

"Sex Piston, I can move—" Stud began, but Sex Piston cut him off.

"Do you love me, Stud?" Sex Piston turned in his arms so that she could see his face.

"Yes, Sex Piston, I love you."

Sex Piston looked down at the ribbons and stuffed rabbit in her hands.

"It's not going to be easy, Stud." She licked her suddenly dry lips before confessing, "I can be a little obnoxious, I have a bad temper, no one likes my friends, and my family is nuts." She raised her eyes to him. "But, I think I'm in love with you."

"I think I can handle all that," Stud said, taking the ribbons and rabbit from her hands and tossing them onto the chair by the window.

Unbuttoning her black sheer blouse, he let it slide down her arms to land on the floor. The silky red cami underneath barely covered her breasts. He tugged her black skirt down her legs before turning her to sit on the bed. Going down to his knees, he took off her high-heeled sandals before staring at the tiny red thong that barely covered the fleshy lips of her pussy.

Sliding the panties down her slightly raised hips, he didn't take his eyes away from the flesh he exposed; glistening wetness anxious for his touch. He pressed brief kisses on the inside of her thighs before he spread her thighs wider, placing them over his shoulders as his mouth went to her pussy, licking the tiny drops of her desire. His tongue slid between her folds before slipping into her opening.

Her moans and cries filled the room as he feasted on her, dragging her ass to the edge of the bed before he unzipped his jeans, pulling out his cock. He took her hips in his hands, pushing her hips downward as he took his mouth away.

Her eyes looked up at him in desire as she slid downwards to his lap, her back now against the side of the bed. His fingers moved, holding her ass and spreading her wide as he slid his cock deep into her.

Sex Piston couldn't prevent the scream that filled the room. Stud leaned upwards, pushing even more of his cock inside her.

"It's too tight, Stud," Sex Piston moaned, trying to wiggle her hips to ease the pressure as he began thrusting his cock deep.

"This isn't going to be easy, Sex Piston." Stud's hands moved her hips up and down, his hands completely holding her weight. Her body was positioned so that he did all the work and the only thing she could do was take the pounding he was determined she was going to have.

"When I get done with you tonight, you are going to know you're mine. I can be an ass, I like things my way, you'll have to put up with three kids that aren't yours, and I'm never going to stop loving you."

Sex Piston managed to grasp his biceps, her orgasm building to a level that had her nails digging into his flesh. His words went through her mind and she relaxed, letting her hands grasp his for support. The cock thrusting inside her slid through her slick sheathe as she gave her body to him, finally understanding this man with those tattoos that she hadn't let herself explore yet.

The skull tattoo on his bicep said loyalty. The one on the side of his chest was a wild horse with a flowing mane, showing his commitment to the Blue Horsemen. The three roses on his chest, each one representing a daughter he would protect. Then there was the saying that had been telling her all along how long he was going to be hers. *To the ends of the earth.*

Chapter Nineteen

Sex Piston hung over the rail, screaming her lungs out. "Go, Stud!"

"Sex Piston, stop." Sex Piston felt Sizzle pull her dress further down over her ass.

Straightening, she hugged her ma. "He's going to win again," Sex Piston yelled, jumping up and down. She was wearing a leather dress that came to the tops of her thighs with high heels. Her garters were just below the bottom of her dress, showing blue bows. Her red hair was pulled back to a high and tight ponytail.

The outdoor racetrack was filled to capacity to watch the regional cup championship. The outdoor racetrack was two point two miles long and had twelve curves that the bikes had to navigate at high speeds. Stud was up against bikers that were as good as him from his region.

He came around that last curve, going so fast that he seemed to be riding his bike sideways. The biker ahead of him eased off for a split second to navigate that last curve. That was where he lost his advantage because instead of slowing down, Stud sped up, winning the race by a fraction of three seconds.

Sex Piston, Killyama, Fat Louise, Crazy Bitch and T.A. all jumped up and down. Meri, and Keri joined in; Aunt Katy had volunteered to stay home with Star who would have been exhausted by the long day at the track.

"Sex Piston, pull your dress down. You're showing all your assets," Sizzle snapped, reaching forward in her seat to tug the bottom of the tight dress down.

Sex Piston threw her mother a frustrated look and then took her seat next to her ma, grabbing the popcorn from her. "Chill out, Ma."

"You're just like your grandmother; she didn't care who she showed herself to either."

"Who are you talking about?" Sex Piston asked, staring at her mother, worried that since she had moved in with Stud and his girls in his huge house that her mother was becoming even more lost to reality. Maybe she was wrong and everything hadn't been going as well as she thought.

"Quit staring at me as if I'm going senile. Your pops and I are doing fine without you, Sex Piston. You come by the house twice a day to check on us. We actually see you more now that you moved out."

Sex Piston's hand tightened on the popcorn, refusing to let Fat Louise have it. "Go buy your own. I almost broke my neck going down those steps in these heels."

Killyama handed Fat Louise her popcorn when she started pouting.

"Sucker." Sex Piston kept eating the popcorn, despite Killyama's glare.

"Your grandmother would have—"

"Ma, you've got to quit talking about your mother. The only thing you knew about her was her first name. That was all the woman who adopted you would let you know, so quit acting like you shared such a great relationship."

Her mother looked around, apprehensively surveying the crowd around them. "Sex Piston, there is something I've never told you. I knew your grandmother. She visited me whenever she was able to, but you're right; I barely

remember her at all. I only know what I read about her."
Sizzle leaned closer to Sex Piston, still keeping a wary eye
out for eavesdroppers. "She was beautiful. She was a star.
That's why we named you after her, our beautiful star."

Sex Piston's hand holding the popcorn halfway to her
mouth dropped the popcorn back into the bucket.

"You named me Norma because you thought I was a
beautiful star, like you thought Diamond was your
precious jewel?"

"Of course, honey. My two babies had to have special
names." Sex Piston felt the hurt that she had held that her
parents cared more for Diamond disappear. It didn't
totally disappear because Diamond was always going to be
a daddy's girl, but she was hoping that the big, ass fifty
inch television that she had purchased for Father's Day
might have him reconsidering giving her that title.

"Stud's done," Crazy Bitch said over her shoulder.

"He kiss her?" Sex Piston asked, getting to her feet and
smoothing down her dress with a wiggle of her hips before
handing her popcorn to Killyama.

"Nope, he took the trophy and stepped away. See, I
told you he learned his lesson," Crazy Bitch said smugly.

The second to last race Stud won, the trophy bitch had
grabbed and kissed Stud, and the asshole hadn't tried hard
to break her lip lock. He went a week watching her dress in
her sexiest outfits without getting any. The last race, a
week ago, he had let the trophy bitch kiss him again. She
almost twisted his left nut off when she gave him his early
morning blowjob in the shower. Her man might be slow,
but he wasn't stupid.

"See you guys Monday," she said to T.A. and Crazy
Bitch, giving Meri and Keri their hugs. They had begged to
spend the night with Killyama and Fat Louise, who were
going to drop them off tomorrow afternoon. Sex Piston
bent down to give Sizzle a goodbye kiss. "Later, Ma."

Sex Piston turned to go down the bleachers then
hesitated before turning back. "Ma, what did you mean

your mother was a star?"

"Shh… I shouldn't have said anything. It could be dangerous to open old wounds. Forget I ever said anything." Her mother returned to eating her popcorn.

"Ma, has Diamond come around, you know, bringing you a little something that you and Pops like to smoke on your Saturday nights?"

Her mother's angry glare told her that she better spend another few bucks on Pops present to add the premium channels to make it up to her.

She gave up on her mother and walked the short path to find Stud.

Stud stood next to Bear, waiting for Sex Piston. Travis Shepherd walked by with a group of the bikers, smiling.

"What are you still hanging around for, Wyatt? I already got the phone number you wouldn't take from the trophy girl. It's too late to change your mind."

Stud laughed, shaking the hand Travis held out to him. They stood talking for several minutes about their machines.

Stud saw it in their eyes when he lost their attention.

"Who is that?" Travis said, making sure the sun glinted on his second place trophy.

Stud didn't turn around, enjoying watching the men's reaction.

"You ready, Stud?" Sex Piston came to his side, her hand sliding around his waist. Leaning up, she took his mouth in a kiss that had him almost handing her the trophy. Her lips broke from his, making him wish they weren't two hours away from home.

"Travis, see you next race."

"Aren't you going to introduce us?" Travis asked, giving Sex Piston a practiced smile that she ignored.

"No." Taking Sex Piston's hand, he gave Bear his instructions for getting the bike back safely.

Sex Piston went to the truck. Climbing in, she slid over so that she could sit close to him. Unlike his first wife, Sex

Piston enjoyed watching him race, but she never gave the other riders the time of day.

She had eventually found out that he wasn't working at Powell's. He was just using his garage to build the custom bike he would eventually sell. His bikes were becoming well known, but he would only sell a couple a year. The one he had won on today was one he had built.

"Stud, do you know who sells Shade his weed?"

Her question had him pausing with the key in the ignition. "No. Why?"

"Because Ma and Diamond are either nuts or high," Sex Piston said, trying not to show him how upset she was getting.

Stud leaned back in his seat, turning toward her. "Why do you think that?"

"Because Diamond brought us all bug out bags yesterday and then Ma just told me that my grandmother was named Norma and was a big star. They have to be getting bad weed, don't you think? They both can't be nuts, Stud."

Stud almost laughed, but stopped when he saw she was getting more upset. "What does it matter if they are both nuts? As long as you're not, that's all that counts." He thought that would make her feel better, but it only made it worse.

Sex Piston threw him a pissed off look. "Because shit like that is heredity."

"What does that…?" This time Stud looked closer at Sex Piston, noticing her breasts were peeking higher out of her clothes than usual. The Star tat she had placed on her breast was more obvious. He could even make out Meri and Keri's names within the half moons on the other side of the star.

"Sex Piston, are you…?"

"I'm trying to tell you I'm knocked up and I'm afraid our baby is going to be nuttier than a fruitcake," Sex Piston wailed.

Stud turned the truck on, putting it in gear.

"We going home?"

"Yes, but first we're going to pay Shade a visit."

Also by Jamie Begley

The Last Riders Series:

Razer's Ride

Viper's Run

Knox's Stand

The VIP Room Series:

Teased

Tainted

Biker Bitches Series:

Sex Piston

The Dark Souls Series:

Soul Of A Man

About The Author

"I was born in a small town in Kentucky. My family began poor, but worked their way to owning a restaurant. My mother was one of the best cooks I have ever known, and she instilled in all her children the value of hard work, and education.

Taking after my mother, I've always love to cook, and became pretty good if I do say so myself. I love to experiment and my unfortunate family has suffered through many. They now have learned to steer clear of those dishes. I absolutely love the holidays and my family put up with my zany decorations.

For now, my days are spent at work and I write during the nights and weekends. I have two children who both graduate next year from college. My daughter does my book covers, and my son just tries not to blush when someone asks him about my books.

Currently I am writing three series of books- The Last Riders that is fairly popular, The Dark Souls series, which is not, and The VIP Room, which we will soon see. My favorite book I have written is Soul Of A Woman, which I am hoping to release during the summer of 2014. It took me two years to write, during which I lost my mother, and brother. It's a book that I truly feel captures the true depths of love a woman can hold for a man. In case you haven't figured it out yet, I am an emotional writer who wants the readers to feel the emotion of the characters they are reading. Because of this, Teased is probably the hardest thing I have written.

All my books are written for one purpose- the enjoyment others find in them, and the expectations of my fans that inspire me to give it my best. In the near future I hope to take a weekend break and visit Vegas that will hopefully be next summer. Right now I am typing away on Knox's story and looking forward to the coming holidays. Did I mention I love the holidays?"

Jamie loves receiving emails from her fans,
JamieBegley@ymail.com

Find Jamie here,
https://www.facebook.com/AuthorJamieBegley

Get the latest scoop at Jamie's official website,
JamieBegley.net